"What Do You Want?"

he asked huskily.

Terri forced herself to concentrate on the sweets.

"If you can't choose, let me decide for you. Chocolate has always been one of my favorites." Eyes locked with hers, he raised the confection to her lips. Succumbing hypnotically to this lesser temptation, Terri took a bite of the dark treat.

"How is it?"

"Delicious," she murmured as it melted sensuously on her tongue.

"Then I'd better try it, too."

She watched as he brought the cake to his own mouth and had some. "It is delicious," he agreed in his deep baritone. "But for me it's even more so, because I know you've already tasted its sweetness." As if opening the gate to forbidden delights, he silently lifted the plate and offered it to her.

Dear Reader:

Welcome! You hold in your hand a Silhouette Desire—your ticket to a whole new world of reading pleasure.

A Silhouette Desire is a sensuous, contemporary romance about passions, problems and the ultimate power of love. It is about today's woman— intelligent, successful, giving—but it is also the story of a romance between two people who are strong enough to follow their own individual paths, yet strong enough to compromise, as well.

These books are written by, for and about every woman that you are—wife, mother, sister, lover, daughter, career woman. A Silhouette Desire heroine must face the same challenges, achieve the same successes, in her story as you do in your own life.

The Silhouette reader is not afraid to enjoy herself. She knows when to take things seriously and when to indulge in a fantasy world. With six books a month, Silhouette Desire strives to meet her many moods, but each book is always a compelling love story.

Make a commitment to romance—go wild with Silhouette Desire!

Best,

Isabel Swift
Senior Editor & Editorial Coordinator

TESS
MARLOWE
Indiscreet

Silhouette Desire

Published by Silhouette Books New York

America's Publisher of Contemporary Romance

SILHOUETTE BOOKS
300 East 42nd St., New York, N.Y. 10017

Copyright © 1988 by Ruth Glick and Louise Titchener

ISBN: 0-373-05402-5

First Silhouette Books printing January 1988

America's Publisher of Contemporary Romance

Printed in the U.S.A.

TESS MARLOWE

lives in Columbia, Maryland, with her husband and children. Her own happy marriage has inspired her to want to write stories of love and romance. She enjoys cats, sailing, cooking and travel.

One

It looks as if this place has been trashed by a commando team, doesn't it?'' Terri Genetti said as she gazed wearily at the bare shelves and empty display cases of her once attractively decorated shop.

"At least Gourmet Unlimited had the most successful going out of business sale in the history of Sommerset Mall," her friend Bonnie Foster observed consolingly.

"Maybe, but the money is just a drop in the bucket, considering the sea of debts that's drowning me." Shoulders slumped, Terri wandered over to a shelf and picked up the one lonely enamel teapot that hadn't been snapped up by the eager bargain hunters. It sported a small black chip in the lid. With a grimace, she tossed the pot in the direction of the trash can.

"Hey, that's perfectly good." Bonnie teetered across the quarry tile floor on her spindly heels and intercepted to make an off-center catch. "Don't throw it away."

"Take it, with my compliments."

Bonnie set the kettle down on the counter, came forward and put a comforting hand on Terri's shoulder. "Hey, kid, don't take it so hard. When all this straightens out, you can open up another store."

"Oh, Bonnie, I've spent three years pouring my life into *this* place. You know how hard it is to find a good location, settle on the right mix of merchandise and build up clientele. Until last year I was living on the edge of disaster. Then, just when it looked as though the shop would make it, this had to happen."

In an uncharacteristic gesture of defeat, Terri slumped down onto a wooden stool and pressed her face into her hands. Long dark hair spilled around her shoulders and all but covered her fine features.

"You aren't crying, are you?" Bonnie asked, looking on in helpless concern.

"No," Terri said with a faint sniffle. The last two months had been hellish, but through it all she'd managed to hold together. Now, with her store an empty shell, she could no longer kid herself that things would somehow work out. Seeing her dreams destroyed this way had brought her closer to the breaking point than she'd ever been. But she was determined to cling to the last shreds of her dignity until she was alone.

"It's after closing hours. Let me take you down to the Brass Rooster and buy you a drink," Bonnie suggested.

"Thanks, but I don't feel up to it."

"I'm not taking no for an answer," Bonnie replied, shaking her headful of bright orange frizz.

Coming forward, she took Terri's elbow, helped her to her feet and pointed her toward the small washroom at the back of the shop. "You've got five minutes to wipe eight hours' worth of combat duty off your face before we storm the Brass Rooster."

Terri was pretty sure she wasn't going to take anything by storm. She also knew her friend wouldn't quit until she'd gotten her way. That was a big factor in the success of Bonnie's fashionably punky boutique, Rainbow Rags. Determination was one of the few things the two women had in common. Their age—twenty-seven—was another. Although their styles and personalities were very different, common goals had cemented a friendship between them. Terri had nursed Bonnie through two broken love affairs. But lately it had been Terri who needed emotional shoring up.

Fifteen minutes later, as they sat opposite each other in the Brass Rooster's dimly lit lounge, Bonnie did her best to offer more support. "It is tough," she said, "to be forced to close your successful franchise because the rest of the company went bankrupt."

Terri took a sip of the strawberry daiquiri Bonnie had ordered for her and nodded numbly. Until the Gourmet Unlimited chain had folded, Terri had expected that she would be doing business in the Sommerset Mall for many years to come. She had even started to think about a second shop. But when the letter had come from the head office, her dreams had abruptly evaporated. To keep the store open, she would have had to buy it from the company. Her credit—based on the national reputation of the parent organization—was stretched to the limit.

Terri had spent weeks trying to find a way out of the mess. But none of her desperate letters or phone calls had had any effect. No one was willing to bend the rules, even for critical situations like hers. First Terri had been forced to find new suppliers. Buying from them had squeezed her bank account dry so that she was unable to pay her store's rent. After several dunning letters, the mall management had given her notice that she was going to have to vacate.

Her brother Tony had been her last resort; she knew he would have lent her the funds if he'd had them. But he was the kind of guy who was either flush or broke, and she'd caught him on the down part of his cycle.

"So what did Patterson say to your last letter?" Bonnie asked, referring to the officious little man who oversaw Sommerset Mall's operations for T. & H. Associates, the corporation that owned a string of shopping centers in the area.

Terri grimaced. "He told me he couldn't change management policy."

"They're all heart, aren't they!" Bonnie set down her own drink and gazed sympathetically at her slim, brown-haired friend. There were shadows under Terri's large green eyes. And the day refereeing what amounted to the death knell of her store hadn't done much for her normally immaculately groomed appearance. A streak of dust smudged the front of her russet turtleneck and coffee-brown suit. The paisley scarf that had struck a brave note early that morning now drooped dejectedly.

"Well, I hope this mess isn't going to stop you from taking advantage of that weekend at Hearthwood," Bonnie reminded her friend as Terri leaned her head wearily against the high back of the wooden bench. Six months earlier she had won a contest for the mall's most innovative store display. Her theme had been an Easter egg hunt. She had spent weeks decorating the eggs herself. Each had been a tiny masterpiece, and the overall effect had charmed the judges.

Terri had been awarded first prize—a weekend at Hearthwood, one of nearby Virginia's oldest and most luxurious resorts.

Although she'd been excited about the honor, her recent troubles had made the prize seem pointless. Now she laughed mirthlessly. "Bonnie, you must be kidding! I don't see how I could possibly enjoy it."

The redhead was horrified. "If anybody needs a vacation from her troubles, it's you. Besides, that weekend is worth hundreds of dollars. You can't just chuck it!"

Terri took another sip of her drink. "Don't think I didn't go to the management office and try to persuade them to credit the value of the prize against my rent. They explained it was a package deal for the winners at their ten malls and they'd already paid.''

''All the more reason to take it out of their hide, then,'' Bonnie insisted righteously. ''If you want to spend the weekend moping, you might as well do it in style.''

''I promise to consider it,'' Terri replied, looking around for the waitress. ''But right now I'm so beat, the only thing I can think about is a hot bath and twenty-four hours of sleep.

The following afternoon, James Holbrook looked thoughtfully at the two-page letter that had been passed on to him by Dave Patterson, the manager of the Sommerset Mall. Since he encouraged the staff of each shopping center to handle its own problems, only the unusually worrisome cases were sent to the company's head office, in Alexandria.

He sighed and studied the signature. ''Teresa Genetti'' was scrawled in angry-looking black letters at the bottom of the second page. Ms. Genetti was one furious woman. She wasn't taking kindly to being put out of business, and he couldn't exactly blame her, judging by the facts she'd set forward in her plea for additional time to make the rent payment.

On the other hand, rules were rules. T. & H. Associates wasn't a charity. A whopping big mortgage loomed over the Sommerset Mall. If the merchants who leased space there didn't make their payments on time, the whole project would be in jeopardy and everyone would lose out.

What was more to the point, T. & H. wasn't responsible for the collapse of Gourmet Unlimited. Teresa Genetti should have been a little smarter about whom she picked for a business partner. She'd made the sort of mistake that spelled the difference between success and failure in the business world.

Jim glanced at his watch. He wasn't the kind of boss who ordinarily took off early on Friday while his employees stayed to finish his work. But this weekend was unusual. When the PR department purchased the package of weekend prizes at Hearthwood, the historic resort had thrown in an extra reservation with his name on it and a brochure touting their new conference facilities. Their ploy was tempting, though there'd been so much work in the office recently that he'd decided to let it go. However, over the past week he'd been reconsidering. He hadn't gotten away in months. Perhaps it was time for a change of scene and a relaxing weekend. He'd been putting off the final decision. Now he realized he'd made up his mind. Oddly enough, it was Teresa Genetti's letter that had done it. It was one more thing he didn't want to have to deal with until Monday morning—one more thing it would do him good to get away from.

Dropping the neatly typed sheets of cream-colored stationery on top of the pile, he pushed back his chair and stood up. After rolling the fatigue out of his broad shoulders, he strode to the door.

"Call Hearthwood and confirm my reservation," he told his secretary.

Ms. Hopkins glanced up from the memo she was typing and eyed her boss with the expression of a mother who's finally gotten her reluctant son to dress up and go to the school dance. "So you've decided to spend the weekend at Hot Springs after all."

"Yup."

"Good for you."

The corners of Jim's keen dark eyes crinkled. He knew this was a forward move in Maggie Hopkins's not so subtle campaign to take care of him. She'd already cut him down to two cups of coffee a day and persuaded him to quit smoking. Now she was attacking him for working late. "I decided I was tired of being chained to this damn desk,'' he admitted.

"Well, I should hope so," she agreed, then paused. "I hate to ask this, but as long as you're going to be there, shall I make arrangements for you to greet the prizewinners this evening?"

Her boss pushed a lock of dark hair off his forehead. "Heck, no! You've been pointing out all week that I need a rest. I'm going to Hearthwood for a vacation, and presumably so are they. Don't you dare arrange for me to do anything but play golf and laze in the pool."

She laughed. "Got it. Does that mean you're going to be traveling incognito?"

"No need for any cloak-and-dagger stuff." He flashed her a grin. "My name probably isn't familiar to the mall merchants, and I certainly don't intend to be drawing their attention."

All the same, as he climbed into his charcoal-gray BMW a few minutes later and pulled out of the company parking lot, he couldn't seem to drag his mind away from business. He kept thinking about Teresa Genetti. He'd have to be a Scrooge not to sympathize with her situation. How old was she? he wondered, and how had her business been faring until this crisis? He should have had Maggie pull her file to fill in the background. Maybe there was some way she could qualify for the special loan program he'd set up two years earlier.

The thought brought him up short. What the hell was he doing? He knew he was a Type A personality, but surely he could turn that side of him off long enough to enjoy the weekend. For the next two days, relaxation was his goal, not finding solutions to business difficulties.

Terri sat staring vacantly out her apartment window at the parking lot below. It was three in the afternoon, and she felt completely at a loose end. She had awakened with a start at eight, thinking she was late for work. Then a picture of Gourmet Unlimited, with its gutted shelves and empty bins, came flooding back. She wasn't going to be opening up her shop this or any other morning. With that realization, it had suddenly seemed pointless to do anything at all. That was easy, since she felt about as chipper as a morgue attendant.

Though she'd been exhausted when she'd crawled into bed the night before, she hadn't fallen asleep until close to five. Instead, during the long, dark hours, her mind had spun uselessly while she tried to come up with some solution to her problems. But none of her ideas seemed to make sense. She wished she could talk to her brother Tony. But he'd left for Florida, and there was no way to get in touch with him until he called her.

The phone rang and she jumped. "Terri?" Bonnie's cheerful voice said on the other end of the line.

"Yes."

"What are you doing home? You should be on your way to Hearthwood by now."

"Oh, Bonnie, let's not start that again."

"I mean it. I know you're just sitting around, brooding. If you're going to do that, you might as well be lolling in a heated pool or lying on a table, letting a masseuse work the kinks out of your muscles. If you don't pack your bags, I'll come over and do it for you."

Terri hesitated. She hadn't even had the energy to get dressed this morning. Now her first impulse was to say no again. But on second thought her friend had a point. She was too drained and dispirited to think positively about the future. Maybe a change of scene would make a difference, it wasn't as if she had something better to do.

"Okay," she told Bonnie. "You've talked me into it."

"You're sure you're not going to just hang up and then crawl back in bed and pull the covers over your head?"

"No, I promise."

"Good. Have a wonderful weekend. I'll expect a full report on Monday."

Surprisingly, turning her mind to something else did help, Terri thought a few minutes later as she took stock of her wardrobe. Making the best of herself on a tiny budget was something she had learned early in life. Now the habit was so ingrained that even with her life falling to pieces, she selected her clothing carefully.

Of course, she hadn't started out looking as if she'd just stepped from the pages of *Mademoiselle*. As a kid growing up in Baltimore's Little Italy, she'd worn her older sister Angela's hand-me-downs, and her haircuts had been strictly back-porch productions. But she'd never been content with second best. She'd gone after a scholarship to an exclusive East Coast girls' college and, to the surprise of her family, won it.

There she'd discovered that outsiders had to make even more of an effort. Academics were important, but appearance also counted for success. She'd found the right cut for her thick brown hair and learned how to complement her clear skin and small, regular features with makeup. She'd discovered that in certain outlets, designer clothes could be bought for a fraction of their original price and that society matrons often discarded barely worn fashions at second-hand clothing shops.

This knowledge had stood her in good stead and still did. When she finished straightening her skirt and looked in the mirror, she was certain that none of Hearthwood's wealthy guests would dream that she'd been raised in an over-crowded row house.

Outside, the fall weather gave a lift to her spirits. I'm not going to think about my problems all weekend, she vowed as she switched the radio to an easy-listening station and rolled down her window. Her destination was less than a two-hour drive away.

As soon as she was out of the metropolitan area, the scenery changed dramatically. Apartment complexes and shopping centers gave way to rolling hills and stands of oaks and maples interspersed with tall pines. In the late-afternoon sun, the brilliant fall colors were very beautiful. They promised that morning in the mountains would be spectacular.

There were no billboards advertising Hearthwood, just a discreet sign on a wrought iron gate that was flanked by a serpentine red brick wall. She turned in, then drove slowly up the winding driveway past serene vistas of ancient boxwoods and stately rhododendrons. Somehow she really did feel as though she was entering another world, where the pace of life was slower. Terri found herself imagining the horses and carriages that had brought affluent guests to this place more than a century ago. As her Nissan rounded a final sweeping curve, she paused to gaze at the sprawling resort.

Someone with baronial pretensions—or a quirky sense of humor—must have designed the place, she thought. Its crenellated embrasures, ramparts and turrets resembled those of a castle. On the other hand its many wings, with their peaked roofs, appeared to sprawl over several acres, so the structure also looked like a series of connected circus tents.

Though it was quite old, the resort had kept up with the times. In response to the contemporary fitness mania, it had installed one of the most complete recreational complexes on the East Coast. Bowling, roller skating, tennis, trap- and skeet shooting, golf, skiing in season and horseback riding were just a few of its offerings. What's more, "healthy living" weekends were available for guests who wanted to shape up and slim down.

Terri had no sooner pulled up at the front entrance than a uniformed attendant whisked away her car while another carried her bags to the front desk. There, however, she encountered a slight hitch. After a profuse apology, the receptionist asked her to wait in the lounge for a few minutes, because her room wasn't quite ready.

Jim Holbrook had arrived a quarter of an hour earlier. "I'm terribly sorry, sir," the red-uniformed clerk said as he checked his computer screen. "Your suite isn't quite ready yet. There'll be a short delay, but we'd like to offer you a complimentary drink while you're waiting." He gestured toward a small lounge area where several people sat sipping cocktails.

Usually impatient with snags of that sort, Jim opened his mouth to protest. Then he remembered his vow to hang loose during this getaway. After all, he was in no particular hurry to unpack.

"That will be fine," he agreed. He turned, then strolled across the carpeted lobby.

After settling into one of several comfortable wing chairs, he ordered a Scotch and water. The service was suitably swift; the drink arrived within minutes. While he sipped at it, he leaned back and glanced around.

The reception area, with its crystal chandeliers, antique sideboards and Oriental rugs, certainly made a pleasing impression. Looking over the scattering of other guests who were presumably also waiting for rooms, he wondered idly if any were prizewinners from one of his malls. Then he pushed the thought away. It didn't matter, because he wasn't planning to meet any of his merchants this weekend. He was reaching for a magazine when a young woman with shoulder-length brown hair walked in the door. His gaze traveled past her, then bounced back like a cinematic double take.

Suddenly he felt like a sailor who'd finally gotten leave after nine months at sea and just encountered his first female. His reaction was uncharacteristic and its strength took him by surprise, making it impossible for him to tear his eyes away.

Eagerly he took in the details of her appearance. She was tall and willowy, with the kind of long slender legs that were made for black lace stockings and delicate high heels with rhinestone straps. Her rich hair was in slight disarray, and he pictured himself letting it curl around his fingers on the pretext of smoothing it out.

As he watched, she hesitated in the doorway, tucking back a strand of the hair he suddenly longed to stroke and looking around as though she were acclimating herself to the elegant surroundings. It was too good to be true to think that such a beauty was here on her own, and Jim waited tensely for a husband or boyfriend to follow her in. Much to his relief, no one did. She approached the desk alone.

Forgetting the glass of Scotch, which his hand was gripping like a life ring, he continued his surreptitious survey. Against the dark green of her suit, her rosy skin glowed like a camellia in bloom. And she was the only flower in the garden. For Jim, all the other guests in the lobby had ceased to exist. Under the influence of a powerful compulsion, he watched while she stood talking to the receptionist.

She must have gotten the same runaround as he had, Jim reflected, because after a brief exchange with the clerk, she walked to the lounge area and looked for a seat.

This way, beautiful lady, he said to himself. There's an empty chair right across from me.

He knew providence was on his side when she walked straight to the wing back he'd been rooting for.

Up close she was even better than she appeared from a distance. Her large, almond-shaped eyes were quite an unusual shade of green, he saw, and her skin was flawless.

For a moment the waiter blocked his line of sight, and Jim had to leash his impatience. But not being able to see her only heightened his appreciation for her other qualities. He heard her ask for a glass of dry Chablis and was instantly taken with the musical quality of her voice.

Then the waiter left, and she shifted slightly so that her skirt drifted just above her perfectly sculpted knees. Jim inhaled sharply and forced himself to let out the breath slowly. It had been a long time since a woman had knocked him completely off his pins—and he wasn't even standing up!

He advised himself to slow down. He'd just scare her off if he came on to her like a bull elephant in mating season. This called for a little finesse.

The drive down from Maryland had been tiring. Terri had pictured herself stripping off her clothes and climbing right into a hot, relaxing tub the moment she arrived at Hearthwood, so she was none too happy about settling for a glass of Chablis in the lobby. She picked up a brochure from the marble-topped table next to her chair and began to flip through the pages. A photograph of guests lolling about in what looked like a South Seas island cave caught her eye. Perhaps that kind of hydrotherapy would do her some good. She quirked her lips slightly at the thought.

"Did I miss something amusing in the Hearthwood sales pitch?" a deep baritone voice inquired.

Startled, Terri lifted her head. Her gaze immediately tangled with that of the man sitting opposite. Dark eyes that reminded her of rich Colombian coffee made her forget about the brochure she was holding. The eyes were set in a face that she found compelling beyond the surface impression of mere handsomeness. *Rugged, individualistic, uncompromising,* were the words that came to mind. But there was more to the impact of their colliding gazes than just that. She was suddenly self-conscious.

How long had this man been looking at her? she wondered. Long enough, she suddenly realized, all her feminine instincts unaccountably galvanized.

Perhaps an impulse toward self-protection brought the most prosaic of words to her lips. "I've never been to a hot spring before," she told him. "I guess I was wondering just how medicinal they really are."

"I expect the medicinal qualities are overrated," he observed wryly. "But I understand that the mineral waters are great for relaxing, and that's what I'm here for," he added, though he knew that was no longer true. Sitting across from this particular woman was making him feel about as relaxed as a fire horse that'd just heard the alarm bell.

"It's the same for me," Terri agreed. "I need to get away from reality." The statement made her think of her shop, and she frowned.

Jim, watching her intently, noticed the change in her expression and wondered what it meant. What sort of reality was she escaping? And would she be willing to let him be part of that escape?

"Well, it looks as if you picked the right place," he observed, lifting his glass. "Are you here alone?" He held his breath.

When she nodded, he smiled and tried not to let his face convey how much was hanging on the answer to his next inquiry. "Me, too. Since we're both on our own, why don't we join forces? Will you have dinner with me tonight?"

Terri hesitated. The question made her realize just how off balance she was. That she hadn't terminated this conversation right at the beginning was one indication. After all, she really knew nothing about this man. He could even be married.

Trying not to be too obvious about it, she glanced at the large, strong-looking hand that rested easily on his knee. There was no wedding band on his ring finger and no telltale white line, either. At least he didn't seem to be a married man out for a little philandering.

Jim had already checked her hand. Now, as he noted her unobtrusive but purposeful scrutiny, he gave her a point for integrity. A lot of women wouldn't care one way or the other whether a wife languishing at home was part of what he was trying to get away from.

There had in fact been no wedding ring on his hand for the past six years. He'd married in his mid-twenties. It had been a real love match. She'd been beautiful and fragile, and he'd enjoyed making sure that she wanted for nothing. But shortly after their third anniversary, a drunk driver had snuffed out Janet's life and almost brought his world to an end. The only way to keep his sanity and hold grief at bay had been to throw himself into his work. The pain had eventually subsided; he was no longer grieving. But spending long hours every day at his desk had become a habit he couldn't shake—one he certainly intended to make an all-out effort to dislodge this weekend.

Ordinarily Terri wouldn't have considered accepting the invitation of a stranger on such short acquaintance. But what had all her years of playing by the rules done for her? she asked herself now. She had turned down a proposal of marriage from a very eligible man so that she could work to build something of her own. Now here she was, three years later, with a ruined store and a bank account as flat as a pancake.

Stalling for time, she took a sip of wine. She might be feeling reckless, but she really wasn't very experienced in this sort of thing.

Jim watched these emotions play across Terri's face. Although they'd only just met, he was surprisingly distressed at the thought that she might turn him down. "Don't agonize over the decision. I really would like your company at dinner, so say yes," he urged.

Again she met his dark gaze. "I'd like that, too," she admitted throatily.

He grinned. "Good. Now that that's settled, maybe we should exchange names."

Terri stared at him in surprise. He was right; they hadn't even introduced themselves. Too late, her cautious streak resurfaced. Did she really want this to be more than a casual encounter? "I'm Terri," she finally replied.

"Jim." All right, if she wanted to play mystery woman and keep things on a first-name basis, it was okay with him for the time being. "Now," he continued, "we only have to decide on what time to eat so I can make a reservation in the Blue Ridge Room," he said, naming the hotel's most elegant dining room.

Terri glanced at the elaborate grandfather clock that stood in front of one of the square marble pillars.

Sensing her uncertainty, he added, "I assume that like me, you're waiting for your room. So I guess it depends on when we can get into them."

At that moment, a bellman came up behind Jim and cleared his throat. "Mr. Holbrook?"

"Yes."

"I have the key to your suite."

Jim smiled at Terri and got to his feet. "This lady," he said, "has been waiting almost as long as I have. Are her accommodations ready yet?" In a way he was glad their tête-à-tête was coming to an end. The fact that she hadn't revealed her last name and her wary expression earlier told him she wasn't the kind of woman who went in for casual liaisons. Now that she'd agreed to meet him for dinner, he knew that it was best to leave while he was still ahead.

"Oh, don't worry about me," she assured him quickly. "I haven't finished my wine yet, and I'm content to sit here for a while longer. I'll meet you in front of the elevators."

"Is seven-thirty okay?"

"Fine."

"I'll be looking forward to it." Smiling again warmly, he raised his hand in a brief salute, then turned to follow the bellman. Terri watched until his tall, broad-shouldered form disappeared. Then she sipped again at her wine. Jim Holbrook. Probably James Holbrook. She tried out the name, strangely pleased with the way the syllables rolled off her tongue. It suited him; the first name straightforward, the last a bit aristocratic. And he certainly knew how to handle women. In less than ten minutes he'd gotten himself a dinner date with her. In fact, now that he was gone, she couldn't help being a little taken aback by herself. Letting a total stranger ask her out like this was really a first. She'd come here to get away from the depression she felt about her ruined business. Well, she'd certainly made a good start!

"Ms. Genetti?" The bellman interrupted her thoughts. "Thank you for waiting. I'm pleased to tell you that your accommodations are ready. Shall I take you and your baggage up now?"

Terri put down her almost empty glass and rose, relieved to be escaping to the privacy of her room.

Two

Ten minutes later, Terri stood surveying her luxurious quarters. She might be angry at T. & H. right now, but she had to concede that they certainly had gone all out for their contest winners. She had expected a nice room. Instead, she would be spending the weekend in an elegant suite that was bigger than her apartment in Gaithersburg. There was a Williamsburg sitting room, and a bedroom that included what looked like a genuine antique four-poster, complete with lace canopy. She'd never slept in a bed like that before. Smiling, she went over and tested the mattress. It was more than large enough for two people, she thought. Suddenly her wayward imagination presented her with a picture of Jim Holbrook lying beside her, his dark eyes warm with desire and invitation. Her physical response was instantaneous. Beneath her silk blouse, she felt her nipples tighten as if to invite the caress of a man's hands—and lips.

Shocked by the reaction, she sprang off the bed. For a moment she stood disoriented in the center of the room, wondering what in the world was wrong with her. She'd met Jim Holbrook only a few minutes ago. How could she be thinking of him like that when she barely knew him? Returning to reality, she went to investigate the rest of the suite.

In contrast to the old-fashioned ambience of the main rooms, the bathroom was very up-to-date, but no less luxurious. Terri had always loved to relax by soaking in a hot tub. This one was going to be a truly sybaritic delight. It was of black marble with gold faucets and big enough for two. Now, why did that make her think again about Jim Holbrook?

As she turned back to the bedroom, Terri pursed her lips. Actually, she mused, it would be wonderful to sink into that huge tub all by herself. Afterward, she could call for room service and watch a little television, then turn off the light and get a good night's sleep.

Recognizing the symptoms of cold feet, Terri shook her head and smiled. After the way Jim Holbrook had invaded her thoughts just now, she was beginning to have serious reservations about keeping their dinner engagement. Maybe the best thing would be to call the man and put him off with the excuse that she was too tired.

She reached for the phone, then paused. No, both she and Mr. Holbrook were going to be here for the duration. She didn't want to ruin her weekend by spending it avoiding him. And for that matter, what was the big deal about dinner with a good-looking man? So he'd found her attractive, and she'd responded. Wasn't that better than moping around and feeling depressed? As long as she could keep things under control, being in his company was a good way to pick up her spirits.

On that thought, she unzipped her garment bag and began to unpack. The mechanical routine was soothing. By the time she had finished, she was feeling more optimistic about the evening ahead.

Grabbing her robe, she headed for the opulent bathroom and its luxurious marble fixtures. She'd never seen a tub equipped with a Jacuzzi. Well, here was her chance to try one out. When she'd filled the tub above the jets, she set the timer, flicked on the wall switch and then sank into the water. In a moment, pulsing streams of warmth began to massage her body, swirling around her breasts and soothing away her tensions. Half an hour later, refreshed by her invigorating soak, she was feeling more like a movie star in a glamorous Hollywood mansion than a failed storekeeper.

After stepping out of the tub, Terri surveyed her slim, high-breasted body in the floor-to-ceiling mirror. She was pleased with what she saw. With a shake of the head, she acknowledged that for the past two years she'd been working such long hours that she'd lost touch with the sensual part of herself.

As she slipped into lacy underwear, she thought about Jim Holbrook and hummed a favorite old love song. Then, with more care than she'd taken in months, she applied flattering but understated evening makeup. She went back to the closet and stood debating between the two dressy outfits she'd brought. Finally, she decided on the silky shirtwaist with a baby leopard print. Though the cut of the dress was conservative, the slightly daring print matched her reckless mood. She was just stepping into strappy high heels that emphasized her trim ankles when the absurdity of what she was doing struck her. She'd been spinning a web of fantasies about a man she hardly knew and who surely couldn't come anywhere near living up to them! He probably wasn't as good-looking as she remembered. Or as sexy, either.

Yes, he was, she thought a few minutes later when she stepped out of the elevator and spotted the tall, dark-haired man crossing the marble floor toward her. She stopped in her tracks. Jim had changed into a dark suit. The formal cut of the expensively tailored outfit brought out his masculine good looks in a new way. Up in her room she'd been responding only to her thoughts about the man. The compelling reality of his presence was a great deal more potent.

Her breath caught in her throat as she took in the warm glint in his dark eyes, which ranged over her in a slow, appreciative gaze that brought a flush to her skin.

"You look terrific," he murmured huskily as he stopped in front of her.

"Thank you," she managed to whisper. It had been a long time since Terri had felt uncertain of herself and out of her depth with a man. But that was clearly the case now as Jim guided her toward the entrance to the Blue Ridge Room. She was much more aware of the firm grip of his large, capable hand on her forearm than she was of her surroundings.

It was a moment before she was even conscious that they had stopped inside the entrance to the restaurant. True to its name, it was decorated completely in blue—from the deep tone of the carpet to the paler shades of hyacinth in the hand-painted wallpaper. The effect might have been subdued but for the spectacular floor-to-ceiling windows that formed one whole wall. They looked out on the majestic mountain range that guarded the valley where Hearthwood nestled. The sun had just set behind one of the peaks, turning the evening sky to a dark red streaked with gold.

"What a beautiful setting!" Terri exclaimed in an attempt to dispel her unsettling reaction to Jim.

"Yes, I thought you might enjoy the view, so I requested a table by the window," he told her.

At that moment, the maître d' caught her companion's eye and inquired about their reservations. He checked his book and showed the couple to a handsomely appointed table overlooking the panoramic vista. After the man had lit the candle in the center of the table, a waiter came over to take their drink orders.

When they were finally alone again, Terri couldn't stop herself from making another comment about the gorgeous scenery.

"I'm the one with the best view," Jim responded, shooting her another warm glance.

The implicit compliment flooded Terri with pleasure and she felt her cheeks grow hot.

Why was she so knocked off balance by Jim Holbrook? she asked herself. Answers came readily. The grinding pressure and cruel uncertainty of the past few weeks had thrown her in so many ways. Now, here she was in this lush fantasy environment, which was completely unconnected with her real life. It even included a darkly handsome stranger—the kind of man every woman secretly dreamed about. Sitting across from him, she found it all too easy to feel as if she were someone else—a woman far more reckless than the real Terri Genetti, who wouldn't hesitate to reach out and grasp all that life offered. Terri was aware that for someone as conservative as herself, this was an extremely dangerous state of mind. But that didn't make the whole situation any the less seductive.

From beneath lowered lashes, she continued to study the man across the table. Their meeting was like the opening scene in one of her favorite old Hollywood movies.

How often does someone like me get to play a role like that? she asked herself. It was like being offered a chance to pretend that all her demoralizing problems didn't exist.

Lifting her eyes to her dinner companion's darker ones, she struggled to find words that would restore her sense of balance. "What do you do when you're not escaping from reality for the weekend?" she asked, wishing the timbre of her voice weren't quite so audibly husky.

Jim hesitated. "Oh, let's not talk about reality. Let's concentrate on what's really important." He reached across the table and laid his hand on hers. "Is there anyone special in your life right now?"

"No." The question and the unexpected gesture had come so suddenly that she hadn't had time to be evasive.

He squeezed her hand and then withdrew his. "I'm glad."

The waiter came with their drinks, and they paused until he went away.

"I was thinking how lucky I am," Jim observed, taking a sip of his Scotch and water, his intense gaze remaining fixed on her face. "A woman as lovely as you isn't likely to be unattached for long. Let's find out what we have in common. How do you like to amuse yourself?"

Terri laughed a shade nervously, partly in reaction to the directness of his approach. "You mean like hang gliding, skydiving, Arctic exploration or big-game hunting?"

His eyes sparkled. "Oh, is that what you do in your spare time?"

"Actually, I don't have a lot of spare time," Terri admitted as she slowly turned the base of her wineglass on the table. "But I like to relax by watching the old romantic movies they used to make."

"Don't tell me you're a Bogart and Bacall fan."

"Yes, and Tracy and Hepburn, Astaire and Rogers, and Van Heflin and Lizabeth Scott," Terri admitted.

"Heflin and Scott?" Jim took another swallow of his drink, thinking fast. Back in his teens and later in his college days he'd been a movie buff. He hoped he could remember enough to play on Terri's interest. Searching his memory, he came up with a film title. "Weren't they in *The Strange Love of Martha Ivers*?" As Jim recalled, the film was an early Hollywood attempt to deal with a woman's twisted psyche. To modern sensibilities, it was an amusing travesty.

Terri grinned. "Mmm-hmm. I rented the video a couple of weeks ago."

"Well, it's always stuck in my memory," Jim said with a shake of his dark head. "I guess we have something in common after all—besides wanting to forget the real world this weekend. I like the old flicks, too—sometimes a lot better than what Hollywood is putting out these days."

Terri nodded in agreement.

They took a few minutes to order their dinners, then resumed their conversation. Terri was amazed and pleased that Jim seemed to know about all the obscure films and actors that she herself enjoyed so much.

"What about Westerns?" he asked. "Do you like those, too?"

"I sure do," she admitted a little sheepishly.

"Who's your favorite star?"

Terri thought for a moment. "I like the strong, silent type—Randolph Scott, for example. But my favorite director was Wallace Kiteredge."

"I thought no one else but me was into vintage Wallace Kiteredge!" Jim grinned, now feeling quite sure of his footing. "Do you remember that marvelous scene in *Mexican Standoff* where Buck Fielding finally crosses the Rio Grande?"

Terri stared at him in delighted amazement. "That's my favorite one!"

"Then we're both in luck," Jim told her. "It's showing at eleven tonight on one of the cable channels." It must be kismet that he'd noticed it in the TV listing this evening, he thought.

The sun outside the huge picture windows had set long ago. Lights were dim in the restaurant, and the flickering candles on the tables cast romantic shadows around the diners. All the couples in the room seemed isolated in their own private spheres of light. That was exactly how Terri felt as she talked with Jim. While they looked into each other's eyes and exchanged their thoughts, they might have been the only two people in the world.

They lingered over dinner, enjoying the conversation and each other. By the time they'd finished their coffee and Jim had taken care of the bill, a small combo had begun playing soft ballads in a corner of the dining room.

"Now, that's my kind of melody," Jim commented as the first haunting strains of "Memories" wafted toward them. He looked inquiringly over at Terri. "Shall we?"

"I'd like that," she said, realizing that she wanted the excitement of being in his arms. Glancing up, she caught Jim's look of anticipation. Had he read her thoughts?

He pushed back his chair and stood up. A moment later he was helping Terri to her feet. Folding her hand firmly in his, he led her to the polished parquet where a few other couples were slowly revolving.

There was a breathless moment; then she felt herself encircled by his strong arms. His steps, like his embrace, were sure and firm, and it was easy for her to follow his every graceful move.

He pulled her closer, making her vividly aware of his lean, hard body. Under other circumstances and with almost anyone else she would have mustered at least a token protest. Instead, she sighed with pleasure, closed her eyes and flowed against him.

"That's right," he rumbled deep in his chest as surely and masterfully he continued to guide her around the floor.

When "Memories" ended, the band followed with another familiar ballad. By unspoken agreement, Terri and Jim stayed on the floor and in each other's embrace. Never before had dancing been like this, she thought hazily. As she matched her movements to his, a tingling awareness spread through her. She'd never felt this intimately involved with a man on the dance floor before. What would it be like to make love with Jim Holbrook?

Were his thoughts echoing hers? she wondered as she felt his hands move sensuously down the line of her back. Terri couldn't keep herself from quivering under his palms. She felt him bend toward her, his lips teasing the sensitive line where her hair was combed back from her smooth brow.

The tender gesture stirred her in a way she found hard to define. She curled the fingers of her right hand more tightly against his while the other stole across his broad shoulder to touch the place where his hair brushed his collar.

When the ballad ended, the musicians announced that they were taking their break. For several heartbeats Terri and Jim stood together on the shadowy dance floor without breaking apart. Then, still not saying a word, he took her hand and led her to the side of the room.

At first she thought he meant to lead her back to the table, but that wasn't the direction he took. Instead, he headed toward a set of double doors. His hand firmly on her arm, he ushered her outside and down several steps. A few moments later, she found herself standing on a secluded terrace below the picture window. An awning cut off the view from the dining room above. The night air was crisp, yet Terri felt anything but cold. Jim glanced around. After assuring himself that they were alone, he guided her into the shadows.

"I don't know about you, but things don't usually happen quite this fast for me," he said gruffly.

She didn't get a chance to pretend that she didn't know what he was talking about. As she tipped her face up toward his, he took her in his arms and pulled her into an embrace much more intense than would have been permissible on a dance floor.

There was something very basic and almost savage about the way his lips descended to claim hers. But Terri's response was no less elemental. She raised her arms with cat-like grace and circled his neck, her leopard-patterned dress straining against her breasts. She laced her fingers behind his head, and after a simmering moment, opened her mouth beneath his. Their tongues met and retreated, twined and dueled. Terri moaned far back in her throat and pressed her body more firmly to his. Never before had she yielded so eagerly to the urgent demand of a man's passion.

The primal response of the woman in his arms was a fiery spur to Jim's own mounting excitement. Holding her close on the dance floor had simply been a prelude. Now he couldn't seem to get enough of her. As his mouth devoured the sweetness of hers, he tangled his fingers in her hair. At the same time, he slid his other hand downward to cup her bottom and pull her thighs more tightly against him, wanting to make her vividly aware of his arousal. Her feminine curves felt wonderful. The crazy thought flashed through his mind that he wished he had more than two hands so that he could caress her everywhere at once.

His whole body was so sensitized to her that even through his shirt and jacket, the pressure of her breasts on his chest was driving him crazy. But suddenly that wasn't enough. He wanted to cup them in his hands, feel their weight, stroke them to aching tightness. Shifting slightly, he raised one hand and brushed the back of it against the silky fabric of her dress.

At that moment a burst of loud conversation from the dining room above them penetrated the sensual fog that was clouding his reason. Terri, too, must have been catapulted back to reality. He felt her stiffen, then she began to pull back. Lifting his mouth from hers, he took several deep breaths. This was madness, he thought. He was acting like a sex-starved teenager.

"Terri, I'm sorry," he muttered against her hair. "But you taste so good."

She looked up at him dazedly, her eyes dilated with passion. And for one insane moment he wanted to pull her back into his arms and start all over again.

Her voice stopped him. She sounded as shaken as he. "I don't feel like myself. I've never done anything quite like this."

His fingers stroked soothingly across her shoulders. "It's not your fault. I brought you out here because I wanted this to happen. I couldn't seem to stop myself."

She shook her head. "No, it was the same for me."

He took another deep breath. "Maybe we should go back inside."

"Yes." She averted her face, and he sensed that she was both embarrassed and confused by her own behavior.

His gaze took in the way her hair had become disordered during their embrace. Gravely he reached down to smooth a dark strand back into place. "Terri, don't let this spoil things between us. I want to spend more time with you this weekend." He laughed self-consciously. "And I promise, from now on I'll be good."

"That's not very reassuring." She straightened her dress. "Maybe the trouble with you is that you're too darn good." The humor broke the tension that had been sizzling between them.

Jim draped his arm around her shoulder and guided her toward the door. "Believe me, this isn't my usual style." He paused and cleared his throat. "Listen, I really do want to get to know you better."

Terri hesitated. Despite what had happened, she couldn't deny her own desire to see more of this man. "As long as it's out in the open and we're with a crowd," she told him. She kept her voice light, but both of them understood the message she was sending.

"We'll talk about that tomorrow. For now, perhaps I'd better see you to your room before you run into any more predatory males."

Terri laughed. They both knew she wasn't likely to run into anyone more predatory than the man she was with. Just then the elevator doors *whooshed* open. They stepped inside.

"What floor?" he asked, his finger poised above the buttons.

"Four," she answered automatically.

When they stepped into the hall, it was deserted. In front of room 415, she stopped to fumble in her bag for one of the plastic cards the hotel issued in lieu of conventional keys.

"I won't pretend I don't want to come in with you," Jim said behind her ear in a husky tone that made her shiver. "But I won't press my luck."

Not trusting her voice, Terri nodded, clutching the rectangle of plastic that represented safety.

"I'll be thinking about you tonight," he continued. "Are you planning on watching *Mexican Standoff?*"

Terri glanced at her watch. Though she felt as if a great deal had happened, it was actually only nine-thirty. "Probably."

"Well, I am, too. So I'll be picturing you enjoying the same treat."

He took the plastic key, his fingers grazing hers, and Terri knew she was just kidding herself if she thought they could start all over again the next day as friendly strangers. Even so brief a physical contact as the brush of his hand made her nerve endings *zing*. The door swung open, and for a moment they stared at each other. She knew he, too, had felt it.

"Good night," he said at last.

"Good night," she whispered back, then virtually fled into the sanctuary of her room. When the door had closed behind her, she waited for the sound of his retreating steps. Hearing nothing, she imagined that he might still be standing there, on the other side of the door, only a narrow barrier of wood between them. Then she recalled that the hallway was deeply carpeted.

Turning away, she automatically began to unbutton the front of her dress. But her mind was not on the task. She was thinking of the awkward words she and Jim had exchanged after their heated kiss. Superficially, it had gotten things back on a more balanced footing. But now that she was alone, she acknowledged to herself how very shaken she felt.

As she slipped the dress over her head, she caught a tantalizing whiff of Jim's after-shave. They had been so tightly entwined on the dance floor and then out on the patio that his fragrance had somehow transferred itself to her clothing. Quickly she hung up the garment and removed the rest of her things.

Usually she went in for no-nonsense nightwear. But the weekend was a special occasion, so she'd dug out and packed an ice-blue satin gown with a matching peignoir that her sister had given her a couple of years ago for Christmas. As she slipped it over her head and let it slither down the length of her body, it felt wonderfully sensuous against her skin. Shivering, she thought once more of Jim Holbrook, then made a determined effort to put the man out of her mind.

After turning back the spread on the four-poster, she climbed into the comfortable bed, plumped some pillows behind her head and settled down with the novel she'd brought.

An hour and a half later she glanced at the digital clock the management had thoughtfully placed on the bedside table. It was almost eleven—time for the Western she and Jim had both been looking forward to. Somehow the idea of the two of them watching it together but separately was appealing.

She slipped out of bed and padded across the thick carpet to the armoire. The TV set was connected to a cable box, and it took Terri several minutes to figure out how to tune in the correct channel. The picture appeared just as Wallace Kiteredge's name flashed across a background of desert, cloudless sky and burning sun. Smiling with anticipation, she settled back on the bed and pulled the spread up around her legs. She'd watched this movie half a dozen times, but not recently. Seeing it again would be like getting reacquainted with an old friend. And it would give her something innocent to talk to Jim about tomorrow.

The movie had been on for perhaps twenty minutes, and Terri was deeply engrossed when a rap at the door broke her concentration.

"Who is it?" she called out, slipping into her robe. As she approached the door, she belted the blue satin around her waist.

"Complimentary champagne," a resonant baritone informed her.

Terri froze with her hand on the doorknob. She knew who that voice belonged to. "Jim?" she whispered.

"Yup. Worst luck. My television set isn't working. I got so desperate that I decided to throw myself on your mercy."

Gingerly, Terri turned the knob and peeked around the edge of the door. Jim was still wearing his slacks and white shirt. But he'd discarded his jacket and tie and opened the top two collar buttons. Gazing quizzically at her, he was standing there holding the promised bottle of champagne and a bag of popcorn from the machine she'd noticed in the lobby.

"Would you be willing to take in a stranded Buck Fielding fan?" he inquired. "I won't be able to sleep tonight unless I see him cross the Rio Grande."

Three

―――

For a full minute they simply stared at each other. Then the force of Jim's presence propelled Terri backward. Mutely standing aside, she watched as he stepped into the suite.

"Very nice," he said, looking around her sitting room and not seeming to notice that she was wearing a clingy silk peignoir over what he must guess was a scanty night dress. "I don't have anything quite this fancy." Through the archway he could see the turned-back spread of the four-poster where Terri had been watching the movie. The sound of Buck Fielding's gravelly voice wafted toward them.

"Around these parts, a man's gotta prove his worth," the hard-bitten cowpoke drawled.

"Will champagne and popcorn do?" Jim asked innocently.

Even though she was self-conscious about her attire and clutched the neckline of her robe, Terri couldn't repress her laughter. "Buck has you pegged. But this is impossible, you know. I'm not going to invite you to loll around on my bed with me watching a cowboy movie at midnight."

"It's only eleven twenty-five," Jim retorted as he consulted the expensive gold watch on his hair-sprinkled wrist. "Besides, we don't have to climb in bed together. I see the high-priced suites have a second television in the sitting room." He pointed to the wall opposite the sofa and then set the champagne and popcorn down on the coffee table. "Do they supply long-stemmed glasses to the fancy digs?"

Jim's invasion of her privacy was insane, Terri thought. He certainly wasn't shy about going after what he wanted. Yet she couldn't muster any more objections. "No, the glasses in the bathroom are just the standard sort—more for rinsing out your mouth after brushing your teeth than for drinking champagne."

"Touché," Jim acknowledged. "But we'll have to make do. Where will I find them?"

"Let me," Terri said quickly, thinking about the lacy underwear that she'd rinsed out and left hanging over the shower rod.

A moment later, as she picked up one of the glasses from the shelf over the marble sink, she caught a glimpse of her image in the mirror. Again she was struck by the insanity of entertaining a man in her suite while she was decked out like an ad for sexy lingerie. She should get dressed again, she decided—then immediately canceled the thought. That would simply be an acknowledgment of her nervousness. Her robe covered her from neck to ankle, after all. Better to take her cue from Jim and try to relax.

After snapping off the TV in the bedroom, she returned with the requested items just in time to hear the loud pop of a cork.

When Jim had turned on the living-room set and poured them each some of the bubbly wine, they touched glasses. Terri glanced toward the small couch. Even though it wasn't a bed, it was far more intimate a setting than she wanted to cope with. Jim seemed to read her mind.

"Since I'm the invader, you can have the couch to yourself," he murmured. Gently he put his hands on her shoulders and pushed her down onto the velvet cushions. "I'd go to any lengths to get to watch this movie," he said, adding a silent *with you*. As he spoke, he turned and settled himself Indian-style on the thick carpet by her feet. Almost at once he appeared utterly absorbed by the picture on the seventeen-inch screen opposite them.

From her vantage point above him, Terri stole a peek at Jim's thick, dark hair. Now that he was in his shirt sleeves, how broad the expanse of his back looked. His position was perfect for her to lean forward and rest her hands on his shoulders, but allowing herself that pleasure would be too much an invitation to intimacy. What was it about this man that captivated her so? she asked herself. A lot of it was a basic response to the components of his personality. She'd been so down this morning. A few hours with Jim Holbrook had changed all that. She'd thought she would never laugh again, yet over dinner she'd been chuckling at his jokes. Even though they'd only just met, she sensed that they had a lot in common. Somehow, being with him made the world seem brighter and full of possibilities.

But there was no way to discount the physical chemistry that had started to bubble the moment they'd set eyes on each other. She had to clasp her hands to keep from reaching out and touching him. It was easy to imagine her fingers massaging the corded muscles of his back. If they had known each other better, that was exactly what she would do, and she knew it wouldn't stop there. But, of course, it was impossible to even think of such a thing. She was embarrassed that the idea had even surfaced in her overactive imagination.

Pressing her own shoulders more firmly against the sofa cushions, she knitted her fingers more tightly in her lap. Yet her eyes kept returning to the man at her feet. He seemed completely comfortable with the arrangement. And she could imagine he'd picked the unthreatening position on the floor to give her the illusion of being in control of the situation.

"Are you comfortable up there by yourself?" he questioned.

"Oh, yes," Terri assured him, although it was far from being true. It was several minutes before she could relax enough to think of watching the film. When she was finally able to take her attention away from Jim and concentrate on the TV, she saw that the wagon train had just survived its first river crossing. Terri had seen *Mexican Standoff* so many times that she was instantly oriented. The next scene would be a humorous interlude around the camp fire.

Apparently Jim was equally familiar with the film. With a knowing grin, he half turned to her and took a sip of champagne. "This coffee tastes like it's three-fourths prairie dust," he said just before the character on screen uttered the same words.

"Then you make it next time," Terri retorted. She lifted her own glass, her words almost in sync with the bewhiskered actor who played Buck's irritable sidekick.

Jim turned to her and applauded silently. "Bravo. I see you like to play the same games."

Were they talking about speaking the dialogue or something else? Terri wondered, but she proceeded as if she had read his comment on only the obvious level. "My brother Tony and I used to go on like that for hours," she admitted, "trying to see who could come out with the most lines before the actors."

"Who used to win?"

Terri grinned. "Usually me."

"Then I won't enter into competition," Jim observed.

"Oh? Whom did you usually play with?"

He gave her a slow, lazy smile. "The girl I went steady with in high school. We spent hours in her parents' den, watching the afternoon cowboy reruns on TV." This was quite true. And Jim thanked his lucky stars that by some twist of fate, Buck Fielding had been his old girlfriend's favorite movie star. As a result, he really did know *Mexican Standoff* backward and forward.

"That's all you did—watch TV?" Terri blurted out the words, then pressed her fingers to her lips. How had *that* slipped out? she wondered.

"Well, actually the activity wasn't all passive," he admitted. "But you probably don't want the details."

"I'll just use my imagination," Terri agreed, backing away from the dangerous topic as quickly as she could. Casting around for a way to change the subject, she spied the bag of popcorn beside Jim on the floor. "Hey, you're hogging that. How about offering me some?"

"Sure," he said, lifting the bag. After their wonderful meal in the Blue Ridge Room, she didn't feel particularly hungry. Nevertheless, she pretended to be enthusiastic about sampling the crunchy treat.

Jim gazed up at her, a quizzical expression on his handsome face. "Now, what could be nicer than this," he murmured, reaching up and giving her hand a quick squeeze. "I don't know about you, but I'm having a wonderful time."

"Mmm," Terri acknowledged. She wasn't sure that "enjoyment" was exactly the word she would use to describe the experience she was having. On the surface, Jim was making a point of being simply companionable, but the vibrations between them were making her all too aware of his very masculine presence. She suspected he wasn't quite as relaxed as he appeared. How would he react, she wondered, if she actually reached out and put her hand on his shoulder, the way she wanted to?

The thought made her pulse quicken. What's more, she had another reason to be on edge. She knew there was a torrid love scene coming up in the movie.

There wouldn't have been a problem with almost any other vintage Western, as most confined their displays of affection to the hero's relationship with his horse. Wallace Kiteredge, however, had been ahead of his time in the sensuality department. The love scene between Buck Fielding and the gorgeous redheaded actress Shannon McLeary had been a sizzler back then, and even now it was pretty hot stuff.

It had fueled many of Terri's teenage fantasies, and she still reacted on a sensual level every time she saw it. How would she feel watching it with this very sexy man so close that she could smell his after-shave? She shot another look in his direction, glad that she was sitting behind him, so he couldn't read her expression.

The scene took place in a cave after Buck had rescued the beauteous and well-endowed Shannon from a landslide.

As the two stars approached the mouth of the cave, Terri tensed slightly and she felt a new tautness in the air. Jim cleared his throat and she flicked her gaze in his direction. He had leaned back against the couch so that his shoulders ever so slightly brushed her leg. He must know what was coming up just as well as she did. Had the scene been part of his adolescent fantasies, also? she wondered. She strongly suspected that it had.

Now was the time for a humorous, offhand comment, Terri told herself. But her throat seemed to close at the thought, and she couldn't dredge up a single witty phrase.

"I've always been an admirer of Shannon Mc-Leary's...acting ability," Jim commented in a way that her feminine instinct sensed was deceptively casual. "And this next scene is one of her best efforts. What do you think?" he questioned, turning his head and studying her expression. She realized that he must be reading her thoughts just as accurately as she was reading his.

Terri eyed the couple on the TV screen. Buck was just pulling an unconscious Shannon out of the rubble where she'd been all but buried. What was left of the starlet's peasant blouse hung from her shoulders by a mere act of will.

"Well, she certainly knows how to handle herself in a man slide—I mean landslide," Terri amended quickly.

Jim's eyebrows rose, but he made no comment about her Freudian slip.

"I was always more interested in Buck than Shannon," Terri hurried on.

"Then you didn't watch this movie as a teenage boy," Jim retorted, confirming her earlier supposition.

They stopped the conversation abruptly as the screen hero swept up his ladylove and carried her to a more sheltered corner of the cave. When he'd taken off his shirt, laid it on the ground and stretched Shannon out full length, he began to check her over carefully—presumably looking for broken bones—although there was nothing particularly surgical about the expression on his face. He was just running his hands lasciviously along her ribs when her eyes fluttered open and she gave a little gasp.

"Makes a man wish he'd gone into the medical profession," Jim commented.

Terri eyed the actor's naked chest. "I don't think he's quite dressed for the part."

"It's the technique that counts."

"Well, most doctors don't get to handle such outstanding patients," Terri fenced.

"Oh, you don't have to be a physician to admire good bone structure." Jim kept his eyes on the screen. But as he spoke, he reached over and laid his hand gently on Terri's ankle, clasping it as though it were a piece of delicately made porcelain.

She drew in her breath as he softly and appreciatively explored the sensitive hollows and ridges. She'd never before considered her ankle an erogenous zone. But Jim was rapidly broadening her experience. She was conscious of every stroke of his slightly rough fingertips on her sensitized skin.

On the screen, Buck pulled Shannon into his arms.

Terri felt a frisson of awareness shoot up her legs so that her thighs trembled. It wasn't just from the sexy scene. The man at her feet whose fingers were now stroking upward, toward the fullness of her calf, was affecting her far more profoundly than the celluloid images that had sparked her imagination in the past.

Terri heard the screen heroine's breathing accelerate. Or was it her own? Her body suddenly felt warm beneath the silken folds of her gown, and she clutched at the peignoir as if the filmy garment could offer some protection from her own runaway responses. This was getting dangerous. She should extricate her leg from Jim's grasp, she thought. But she couldn't move. Instead of looking at Jim and delivering a rebuke, she kept her gaze glued to the screen, where Buck and Shannon were now clasped tightly together. Her mind was still on Jim.

He, too, was only feigning interest in the film. As the love scene had become more exciting, he had sensed Terri's physical response. He remembered the way she'd felt in his arms and the alluring scent of her aroused body. Now the heat of her skin once more brought out the tantalizing fragrance that seemed to trigger an answering male hunger in his own body.

He hoped she wasn't simply caught up in the performance of the screen lovers. He'd met this woman only hours before, but it was as though he'd been looking for her all his life. He wanted her response to be to him as well as to the provocative duet being acted out before them—for there was no question that he was responding to her. As if to assure himself, he let his fingers trail up to the tender place behind

her knee and was rewarded by the sensation of her leg
trembling beneath his touch. Again her barely masked excitement fueled his own.

He had been kidding himself if he thought he could come
in here and share a movie and a bag of popcorn and want
nothing more. As if of its own accord, his hand strayed
around to the smooth contours of her knee. This time, he
thrilled to the sharp intake of her breath. Yet when he stole
a glance in her direction, her gaze was still fixed on the
screen with a tenacity that bordered on desperation.

Even though Jim understood her reluctance to acknowledge the emotions they were both experiencing, he was also
challenged by it. The conquering male in him needed a sign
from her—needed her surrender.

At that moment she looked down and caught his smol-
dering regard. She moved her hand to his as though to still
its motion. But the pleading heat in her eyes sent him another message altogether. Neither of them spoke. It wasn't
necessary.

Her gaze seemed to melt beseechingly into his, and every
detail of her lovely face imprinted itself on his brain. There
was a delicate flush on her ivory cheeks. Her moist lips were
parted, as though begging for his kiss. And her long, dark
lashes were half lowered in a dusky screen, adding mystery
to the depths of her emerald eyes.

There was no mistaking her unspoken invitation, and his
heart leaped at the realization that she shared his excitement.

"Terri," he rasped. Then he was reaching up toward her
to pull her down with him on the rug. She came to him in
one fluid motion, her robe swirling around him in a silken
net. Clasping his arms about her, he leaned back so that her
body was locked intimately against his.

He put his hand on the back of her head and brought it
down so that their mouths could meet. They melded together with all the heat and intensity that had been building

throughout the evening. In the dimly lit room the TV flickered, forgotten. The staged passion between Buck and Shannon was simply a pale shadow of the searing reality that locked Terri and Jim together on the luxurious carpet.

His mouth plundered hers, and she responded with equal fervor. The taste of him and the silken thrust of his tongue were intoxicating. Only the need to draw breath finally ended their hungry kiss.

"Sitting at your feet has been torture," Jim groaned, helpless to keep himself from covering her face and throat with even more heated kisses. At the same time, he slid his hand urgently down her back and over her rounded derriere, pressing her more firmly against his bowstring-taut length.

She gasped as she felt the insistent thrust of his aroused masculinity. Yet far from wanting to draw away, she was impelled to press herself closer, trying to assuage the answering ache of emptiness that had been kindled in her own being.

"Terri," he whispered again, caressing her softly rounded bottom. "So good. This is so good."

It was the same for her. But Terri was past the point of being able to express herself in words. The feeling of Jim's hands on her and his hard body beneath hers set her blood pulsing with such force that she felt light-headed with desire. All at once she couldn't get enough of the touch, the taste, the essence of this man. She moved her hands restlessly up and down his sides, unmindful that her nails were digging into his flesh through the fine cotton fabric of his shirt. Avidly her lips sought his again.

Through the haze of his own spiraling need, Jim sensed her abandon. He wanted to get up and carry her into the bedroom. But he remembered how voices from the dining room had intruded on their passion earlier. If he broke the heated mood between them now, she might withdraw all over again, and he didn't think he could bear that.

He wanted, needed, more of her. He would go mad if he didn't have more. Urgently he shifted her weight, pressing her firmly against his throbbing hardness.

She moaned deep in her throat, her legs opening to sandwich his. Of their own accord, her hips began to move importunately.

"Terri, Terri, Terri," he chanted so low in his throat that it was almost a growl.

With jerky, uncoordinated motions, he unbuttoned the peignoir. After sliding the loosened garment from her shoulders, he slipped the thin straps of her gown down over her arms, revealing the tops of her creamy breasts. Mindlessly she levered herself up so that his lips could feast on their softness.

The twin sensation of his heated mouth against her naked breasts and the throbbing pleasure where their lower bodies were pressed together drove her completely beyond the point of rational thought. All she could do was close her eyes and savor the thrilling tremors of delight that coursed through her.

Jim, too, was caught by the galvanizing fires of the moment. The sweet taste of Terri's naked breasts, the frantic rocking of her body against his, drove him closer and closer to the point of no return. This wasn't what he had imagined between them. But he was helpless now to stop the inevitable.

He heard Terri draw in her breath, felt her body stiffen as she reached the peak of her excitement. And in response, he followed her.

When the scorching wave of heat finally receded, he looked up questioningly into her flushed face. The moment she became conscious of his scrutiny, she squeezed her eyes shut.

Wordlessly, he stroked a coaxing finger along her cheek.

"I'm sorry. I can't imagine what you must think of me."
Her voice was so low that he could barely hear it, even
though his face was only inches from hers.

There was a deep rumble in his chest. Despite her embar-
rassment, she snapped her eyes open. "Are you laughing at
me?" she demanded.

"No, at myself. I haven't done anything like that since I
don't remember when."

"You?"

This time it was his turn to feel a hot stain spread up his
neck. He nodded.

For a long moment, neither spoke. Finally, Jim cleared
his throat. "Believe it or not, I don't normally lose my cool
on quite this scale."

He rolled to his side, taking her with him. At that moment they both realized that her bodice was pooled around
her waist. Slowly Jim slid the straps up her arms. When the
gown was back in place, he lifted the sleeves of the peignoir
and began to maneuver the tiny buttons closed. Seemingly
all his concentration was bent to the task. Not knowing what
else to do, Terri waited until he had finished.

"You know," he said after her garments were once more
put to right, "I wasn't being quite honest a moment ago. I
do remember the last time something like this happened before. I was sixteen and in the back seat of a car at a drive-in
movie. I was with a girl I'd been fantasizing about for
months."

He paused, and Terri held her breath, waiting for him to
finish the story.

"Afterward, I was so embarrassed that I couldn't look
her in the face. I never took her out again." As he finished
the confession, he gazed directly into Terri's eyes. "At sixteen I had to run away from what might have been a close
relationship because of a silly thing like being embarrassed
by my physical response to a beautiful female. But I'm
thirty-seven now, and things are a hell of a lot different. It's

been years since I've met a woman who affects me the way you do."

She nodded gravely. There was no denying the effect Jim Holbrook had had on her.

"Much as I'd like to hold you in my arms tonight, I have the feeling you'd rather sleep alone. But I hope you will be ready to see me tomorrow. I want to have breakfast with you—and lunch and dinner. We may have just met, but what we've found together is very rare. And despite what just happened, it goes beyond sexual attraction for me. I won't deny there's some very potent chemistry between us," he elaborated. "But neither one of us would have reacted the way we did just now if it weren't more than that."

"I thought that, too," Terri admitted, her gaze dropping so that her eyes were hidden by her lowered lashes.

"Then let's spend the day together tomorrow, getting to know each other a lot better."

"I'd like that."

Jim helped her to her feet, then looked ruefully at the TV set. Buck Fielding was galloping into the sunset with Shannon balanced in front of him on the saddle. "Well, so much for my burning desire to see that film," he said with a chuckle.

Terri joined him. "I guess we both were pretty distracted. Maybe next time."

His expression was suddenly serious as he rested his hands on her shoulders. "There really will be a next time. Let's start working on it tomorrow." For a fierce moment, he pulled her close. Then he stood back to say, "I'll let you sleep late. Breakfast at nine?"

"Fine."

"I'll pick you up here."

"Yes." She watched as he closed the door behind him. When he was gone, she stopped the trembling of her legs by sinking to the couch. For the moment she felt almost too weak and shaken to think about walking the few feet to the bedroom. Despite her lingering chagrin over what had happened between them, the idea of spending the night with his arms wrapped around her had been all too tempting. If he'd wanted to stay, she wouldn't have been able to deny him. But he was giving her the space she needed, and she was grateful—and already looking forward to the next morning.

Lost in thought, Jim headed down the corridor toward his room. Although he'd done some fast talking to get into her room, he hadn't been spinning Terri a tall tale when they'd parted. Every word he'd spoken had been the absolute truth. He felt almost as though he'd stepped beyond some invisible barrier into a new world. For a world with a woman like Terri in it was altogether new. Suddenly he stopped, a startled expression on his face. He didn't even know her last name, or anything substantial about her, for that matter. And so far, she hadn't offered to enlighten him. He could tell she wasn't accustomed to getting involved with strangers. What if she changed her mind and slipped away tonight? His heart contracted painfully in his chest as he realized that he'd never be able to find her.

At least he had to know her name. Glancing at his watch, he saw that it was twelve-thirty—not the usual time for acquiring that kind of information. What's more, he knew that after the parting scene between them, he couldn't go back to her suite. Yet somehow he had to know who she was, and he had to know now.

Hurrying to his own room, he picked up the phone and called the front desk. "I need to leave an important message for room 415," he said.

"Yes, sir," the clerk answered as if such requests were common at this hour.

"I haven't got the name quite straight," Jim improvised. "It's a Ms. Terri—" He paused. "This note is blurred and the writing is almost illegible."

"I can help you with that. It's Teresa Genetti."

Instantly the name struck a chord in his memory. He'd been staring at that signature just this afternoon. "Teresa Genetti," he repeated slowly. "Are you sure?"

"That's who we have in room 415. Perhaps you've made a mistake."

Jim felt as if the breath had been knocked out of him. "Perhaps I have." Slowly he replaced the receiver and sank down to the edge of the bed, staring off into space. Teresa Genetti was the woman who had written him that angry letter—the woman he was about to put out of business. What leering fate had played such a trick on him? he wondered. But the bigger question was—what in the world was he going to do about it?

Four

———

They were still entwined on the floor, but somehow they had turned over so that she felt the delicious weight of Jim's body pressing her into the rug. Little tremors of pleasure and excitement rippled up and down her limbs, but when she reached out to clasp her arms around his neck, there was nothing there.

Terri stirred restlessly. Her eyes were still tightly closed, but her hands fluttered out to search the bed for Jim's warmth. She didn't find it, and gradually the realization came that she'd been dreaming. She opened her lids and looked hazily around the opulent bedroom. Slowly, it all came back—Hearthwood, dinner last night, the devastatingly attractive Jim Holbrook appearing at her door with champagne and popcorn. And then their frantic tussle on the carpet in front of the television set.

"Oh, my God," she moaned, and pressed her fingers against her face. Could she have dreamed all that, too? But even as the thought surfaced, she dismissed it. No, it had all happened. How or why, she wasn't quite sure. But it had been real enough.

Terri slid the pillow up against the headboard and propped herself up against it, pulling the downy quilt protectively around her shoulders. Then she glanced at the clock on the bedside table. It was after eight. Hadn't Jim told her he would meet her for breakfast in less than an hour? Terri's eyes widened. She had only forty-five minutes until he would appear at her door again. Did she really want to see him? she wondered, reaching for the bedside phone.

Casual intimacy was not her style. Usually it took her a long time to get to know and trust a person. Bruce, her former fiancé, had asked her out half a dozen times before she'd even agreed to date him. And she'd made sure their relationship had progressed in slow, comfortable stages. Even so, she'd been wearing an engagement ring before she'd finally realized that it wasn't going to work out. He was the kind of man who needed to smother a woman to make himself feel superior. She simply hadn't been capable of being the wife he wanted.

Jim showed signs of being the managing type, too. She recalled the way he'd choreographed last night. On the other hand, he was the most exciting male she'd ever met.

Instead of picking up the phone, she brought a knuckle to her mouth while she tried to think clearly.

Why was she making such a fuss about this? She had only another day and a half here at Hearthwood. Why not just relax and enjoy whatever happened next? Maybe a completely out of character fling was exactly what she needed.

The last advice Tony had given her before he'd left for Florida was "Lighten up, Sis." Maybe she should do exactly that. Only from now on, she'd better mix more caution with her enthusiasm. Which certainly meant that when Jim arrived, she'd better be fully dressed.

Terri leaped from under the covers, scampered across the floor to the closet and slid open its doors. After pulling out a pair of navy slacks, a narrow eelskin belt and a pink silk blouse, she laid them across the bed. Then she headed for the shower.

When a firm knock sounded on her door, she had just finished applying a light dusting of blusher. A little apprehensively, she walked out of the bedroom, self-consciously closing the door behind her. As she crossed the sitting room, she couldn't help glancing at the rug where she and Jim had played last night's little scene. Today she'd originally planned to invite him in for a moment, but she changed her mind.

"Just a minute," she called, and grabbed her purse. When she opened the door and stepped out into the hall, she almost collided with Jim.

He stepped back with a quizzical look. "You must be awfully hungry this morning."

"Starved," she told him, and felt her cheeks turn pink as she closed the door and heard the lock click. No matter what intellectual decisions she'd made this morning, she wasn't very good at playing the sophisticated lady. Trying her best to seem cool and collected, she looked up into his dark eyes and smiled tentatively.

He smiled back, but there was a question on his face. "Terri, are you still feeling embarrassed about last night?"

The question took her so much by surprise that she replied with unintended honesty. "Yes."

"You don't have any need to be."

She didn't answer but preceded him down the hall to the elevator. As Jim followed a pace behind, he admired the dark cascade of her hair and the gentle sway of her hips. Though he could no longer see the way her pink silk blouse draped over her breasts, he could still remember it vividly. And even more clearly he recalled the passion in her beautiful green eyes last night. Why the hell had he made that midnight call to the desk? Things were already difficult enough between them. He hadn't needed another obstacle. But there was no way out of it. He was going to have to tell her who he was and hope she didn't get up from the table and march right out of his life.

Not yet ready to make his revelation, he said conversationally as they stepped out of the elevator into the lobby, "I was jogging this morning."

She turned to him in surprise. "Jogging? On vacation?"

He gave her a lopsided grin. "I was up anyway."

"Oh?"

Jim ignored the implied question. She probably knew that thoughts of her had kept him tossing in his unfamiliar bed much of the night. "It's a gorgeous morning. Why don't we have breakfast on the patio?"

"All right. Sounds good."

He took her arm, enjoying the feel of the cool silk against his fingertips, and they proceeded to the French doors that led to a flagstone terrace overlooking the pool. Blue awnings shaded the tables, which were set with emerald-green cloths and crisp white napkins. In the background, the rolling hills blazed with fall color.

"This is lovely," Terri commented. She took a deep breath of the clean country air. "Now I really am hungry."

"Good, because the buffet looks fantastic."

"You've already investigated?"

He grinned. "Actually, I snitched a blueberry muffin on the way back from my jog."

A waiter came over to pour coffee from a silver pot and then they joined the short line in front of the long white tables. In truth, Terri didn't usually eat much first thing in the morning. But today the scrambled eggs, crisp bacon, sautéed apples and homemade muffins looked wonderful. By the time she'd taken a portion of everything she wanted, her plate was loaded.

When they returned to their table, they both dug in with gusto. As Jim cut a piece of sausage, he looked thoughtfully across at his companion. "You know," he began, "I said last night that I didn't want reality to intrude on this weekend. But I'm feeling quite different about it this morning."

Terri glanced up from her eggs. "What do you mean?"

"Last night I couldn't get you out of my mind. Suddenly I realized that I didn't even know your last name."

An amused smile flickered at the corners of her lips. Actually, as she sat across from Jim she'd been thinking how comfortable and right this seemed—as if she'd been having breakfast with him for ages. But that was just an illusion, she reminded herself, and she had decided that this weekend was going to be a much-needed escape from reality. "That's right, isn't it?" she said aloud. "I'm a lady of mystery."

Jim waited for a moment. When she didn't say anything else, he cleared his throat. "Well, are you going to end the mystery?"

Terri considered the question, torn between her desire to get to know Jim better and her own need for anonymity. Finally her original resolve won out. "No, I don't think I am. I rather like the fantasy element."

Despite the lightness of her tone, the remark stung, and Jim couldn't hold back the sharp retort that sprang to his lips. "That must mean you're not very serious about what's happening between us."

Terri laid down her fork. "Jim, I'm sorry. I didn't mean it that way. I don't know if I can explain this to you or not. I'm not usually like this, but right now there's a lot happening in my life that I can't handle and it's making me—" She stopped, not knowing exactly what she wanted to say. Finally she sighed. "You may not believe it, but I won this weekend here as part of a promotion."

"Oh, I believe it," Jim interjected, thinking that this was the perfect opening to tell her about his connection with her problems. But she was so wound up that she talked right through his remark.

Too caught up in the irony of her own situation, Terri didn't hear the irony in his voice. "It was a prize for the best Easter display window at Sommerset Mall. But since then I've lost my store."

"Do you want to tell me what happened?" Jim asked, feeling rather hypocritical, since he already knew.

"I opened up a branch of Gourmet Unlimited, and I was doing fine until the company went out of business and I couldn't qualify for a loan to buy my stock."

Jim murmured sympathetically.

"You can imagine how depressed I felt. I wasn't even going to bother to collect the prize. But I think if I hadn't, my friend Bonnie would have tied me up and put me in the car."

"Bonnie?"

"Yes. She owns a dress boutique next to my gourmet shop. Or maybe I should say my former shop." She gave a brittle little laugh. "I was so proud of that place. It was all mine. I'm the youngest child in a family of six, and I'm the one who always used to get the leftovers." Briefly Terri thought about her family. Of all her brothers and sisters, the only one she felt close to was Tony. Too bad he wasn't the steady, reliable type.

Jim nodded as he thought of his own childhood. It had been quite different, but the emotion in her voice made him understand how she felt about always being last in line. "Sounds like the shop meant a lot to you."

"More than I can put into words. You just don't know what I've been through over the past few months," Terri continued. "When Gourmet Unlimited pulled the rug out from under me, I was determined not to give up. But those cutthroats at T. & H. Management wouldn't even give me a chance to show them what I could do on my own.''

Uncomfortably Jim took a sip of his cooling coffee. This was not the way he had anticipated telling her he was the president of T. & H. And although Terri was oblivious to the people at the surrounding tables, she was speaking so loudly and heatedly that many of them had turned their heads in her direction. Among them were probably other winners of the display window prize. Jim hoped fervently that no one recognized him.

''I'm sure they're not that bad—'' He began speaking quietly, hoping that Terri would follow his example.

Her head snapped up. ''And just what do you know about it?''

He shifted in his seat. ''They're pretty well thought of in the business community. I actually own some shares of the stock.'' In fact, it was fifty-one percent.

Terri was in no mood to listen to any defense of his company. ''Well, let me tell you some things you may not know. Maybe it's good business practice to make cash flow the bottom line. But I think in the long run, if people don't count for something, a business isn't worth a hill of beans.''

With that she launched into a ten-minute harangue that made Jim's ears burn. Although her picture of his firm was distorted, he could see that Terri's emotions were running so strong that there was no hope of changing her mind here at this breakfast table. And he suspected that even if he gave her the facts, she wouldn't assimilate the information. What a trap he'd gotten himself into! If he told her now that he was the president of the company, she'd probably throw what remained of her breakfast at him.

Terri stopped talking and looked contritely across the table at him. ''Oh, Jim, I'm sorry. This is supposed to be a vacation, and here I am yelling at you like one of the Furies about problems that you can't solve.''

Jim swallowed and stared down at his congealing eggs Benedict, afraid that somehow she might read his face. "Oh, I think I understand," he mumbled.

"No, I don't have any business ruining your morning," Terri declared. Straightening her shoulders, she fixed a smile on her face. "What's the point of having a fantasy weekend if you bring your problems along?"

"That's what you were trying to tell me before we got off on the wrong track," Jim allowed, swallowing his frustration. More than anything else in the world he wanted to get to know this woman. Yet she had just declared most of herself off limits. Somehow he was just going to have to overcome that.

Terri took a slow sip of her cooling coffee.

"Let's see if we can't get ourselves back on the right track," Jim suggested heartily, offering her his most charming smile. He had decided last night that he didn't want to take a chance on losing Terri. He had unfortunately discovered this morning that the quickest way to do that would be to tell her who he really was. Well, part of his business success came from his sense of timing. Now was the time to woo Terri, not tell her the truth. There would be plenty of opportunity for that later. The trick would be in figuring out the proper moment.

Terri's answering smile was brilliant. "Thank you for understanding."

He reached across the table and laid his hand over hers. "It sounds as if what you need is some tender loving care, and I'm just the guy to provide it."

"Oh? Just what did you have in mind?"

"Well, not watching television, certainly."

Their eyes met as they both thought of what had happened between them the night before.

"I meant it's too beautiful a day to spend indoors," he qualified, his voice husky as he hatched a plan. "Why don't

I pick you up in an hour, and we'll do a little genteel hiking."

"That sounds wonderful," Terri agreed. "But why don't we just leave now?"

"Oh, I have a few things to take care of before I can get away," Jim answered mysteriously.

Terri agreed. After she and Jim parted, she took the time to tour the athletic facilities and familiarize herself with the hotel's layout. She was about to go look at the recently constructed underwater grotto featured in the brochure when she saw that it was getting close to the time she was to meet Jim, so she hurried upstairs to put on sneakers and jeans. Lucky she'd thought of bringing them, she told herself as she closed the Velcro fastenings on her shoes.

Jim was a few minutes late, but when she opened the door, he had a broad smile on his slightly flushed face. "All ready for the great outdoors?" he asked as he took her arm and led her to the elevator.

"I guess so. But what in the world have you been doing? You look as if you've been running a race."

"Things were a little more complicated than I anticipated," he said, then changed the subject. "I can't wait to get outside again. It really is pretty around here."

"And autumn is my favorite season," Terri added.

"That's why I arranged the spectacular leaves for you."

Terri laughed.

A few minutes later she and Jim were ambling along a mulch path lined with tall, flaming sugar maples and deep red dogwoods. The woods were cool and silent. The night before, when Terri had made it clear to Jim that the time they spent together should be in public places, she'd meant it. Now she was secretly pleased that the woodland path he'd chosen, while theoretically public, was really quite private.

"How pretty your leaves are," she observed brightly, reaching out to touch a golden-yellow one. Then she stopped and examined the small tree more carefully. "That's strange. This shrub has three different shapes of leaves."

Jim laughed. "I guess you've never camped around here. That's a sassafras. And it's not a shrub. It's a small tree." As he spoke, he reached out and snapped off one of the leaves. He crushed it between his thumb and finger and held it up to Terri's nose.

She sniffed the pungent fragrance appreciatively. "I carry sassafras tea in my shop—I mean my former shop—but I never knew where it came from."

He looked meditatively at his open palm and then brushed his hands together so that the crushed bits of sassafras fell to the ground. "The tea is from the roots. We used to brew it on Boy Scout camp-outs. That and picking wild blackberries made us feel as if we were living off the land—although we always had a big cooler full of soft drinks and hot dogs, too."

Terri noted the sudden, secretive grin on his face. "What are you thinking about?" she questioned.

The grin widened. "I'm not sure I ought to tell you."

"Well, now you have to, don't you?"

He laughed. "Okay. I'm afraid we Boy Scouts weren't always clean in thought, word and deed."

"Oh?"

"Now I'd really better tell you, hadn't I. Sometimes there'd be a Girl Scout troop at the next campsite. Sneaking up on them at night with flashlights in the hope of catching them in their underwear was always the high point of the weekend."

"Oh, I see." Terri laughed. "And how did the girls respond?"

"With squeals and giggles. And one time in retaliation they snuck up on us and threw a bucket of cold water inside our tent."

"Gee, that sounds like good, clean fun."

"Oh, it does, does it? I see you have a warped sense of humor—just like me."

Terri shrugged. "Maybe it's envy. I always wanted to be a Girl Scout. When I was a kid, they'd wear their uniforms to school on the days they held their meeting. I was dying to be one of them, but I always had to go straight home and help out in my parents' grocery store."

So she came by her interest in edibles naturally, he thought. Under other circumstances he would have voiced the observation aloud, but they had made a pact—and he certainly didn't want to cause her any distress again.

"At least you were given a sense of responsibility early in life."

Maybe that explains my behavior this weekend, Terri thought. Latent adolescent rebellion. Aloud she said, "Yes, but I never had much fun."

"Then I'll try to make up for that," Jim said.

His words were too close to her thoughts for comfort. He reached down to take her hand, but before he could make the contact, Terri was pointing toward the purple line of the mountains, which were framed by scarlet maples. "It really is gorgeous around here," she observed.

"Yes, it is," he agreed, settling for dropping his arm lightly around her shoulders.

As they strolled, Terri asked frequent questions about the foliage.

"Oh, look at that!" she exclaimed, starting toward a spot off the path that was carpeted with a brilliant red ground cover.

She was about to reach for a fiery leaf when Jim grabbed her arm and pulled her back. Startled by his abrupt action, she turned and looked at him questioningly.

"You really are a city girl, aren't you?" he said without releasing her.

Her gaze remained fixed on his strong masculine features. "What do you mean?"

"You were about to pick a bouquet of poison ivy. Believe me, that would have been a sure way to ruin your vacation."

Terri glanced over at the beautiful patch of foliage. "It looks so lovely and innocent."

"Sometimes things that look innocent are dangerous," Jim murmured. As he spoke he wrapped his arms around her and pulled her back against the length of his strong body.

Terri couldn't repress a little shiver of excitement. "Then I guess I'm lucky you're here to protect me," she managed to say.

"Mmm." As they stood there under the leafy canopy, he tightened his hold and nuzzled his lips against the soft skin at her hairline.

Terri was tempted to stay there, but she wasn't accustomed to giving in to temptation easily. "There is such a thing as overprotection, though," she added, pushing herself gently but determinedly out of his arms.

Without waiting for his reply, she headed off down the path again. Jim watched the set of her shoulders and knew that he was trying to push things too quickly between them again, but he couldn't seem to help himself.

She was twenty-five feet ahead when she came to a division in the path. Automatically, she started to take the right.

"Not that way," Jim called.

He certainly liked to take charge of things, Terri found herself thinking again as she turned and looked back. "Does it matter?"

"I suppose not. But I can hear a waterfall off to the left, and I thought it might be fun to go down and see what it looks like."

Terri stood still and listened. Jim must have awfully sharp ears, since she could just barely make out a sound that might be cascading water. However, she allowed him to steer her in the direction he had indicated.

As they walked on, the sound became more distinct. A few minutes later Jim pointed to a side path that led down a slight embankment. When they broke free of the trees, they were at the edge of a stream. To their left was a sheer rock face where a pretty little waterfall plunged into a deep pool of dark water.

"Oh, what a marvelous setting!" Terri exclaimed. "It makes me think of wood nymphs and panpipes." She cocked her head and listened for a moment. "In fact, there is a sort of musical sound that I can hear. What is it?"

He was silent, too. "Not panpipes. Crickets."

Terri wrinkled her nose.

Jim laughed. "If you don't like bugs, think of these crickets the way they looked in that old Disney cartoon— with violins ready to serenade us at lunch."

She grinned back at him. "I like the image that conjures up. Obviously it wasn't just the same westerns we watched when we were kids. But you're joking about lunch, aren't you?"

"No joke," he said, taking her hand and leading her toward a flat rock that projected into the pool. He knelt down and pulled up a rope that she hadn't noticed. She saw, to her amazement, that it was attached to a bucket that held a bottle of wine.

"I hope you like sauvignon blanc." Jim turned to her with a self-satisfied grin on his face and an icy bottle in his hands.

"It depends on the year," Terri replied.

"Listen, lady, I'm quite proud of my knowledge of wine. Don't tell me it's going to turn out that you know more than I do."

She shrugged. "Well, I did grow up in an Italian household. And making recommendations to customers was one of my specialties." She reached out and took the bottle from him. "This does look like a good year, by the way." Despite her tongue-in-cheek remark, the implications of finding the bottle here stunned her, and suddenly she understood why her companion's face had been flushed when he'd picked her up. "Jim, you didn't really come all the way down here after breakfast just to hide that bottle, did you?"

"Nope." He pushed aside a cover of brush and pulled out a wicker picnic hamper.

Now Terri really was astonished. "Where in the world did you get that?"

"The hotel packs lunches for hikers. It was just a little extra trouble to get the basket—and persuade them to fix something a bit more imaginative than trail mix."

Speechless, Terri watched as Jim spread a blanket on the rock and began unpacking the basket. She was both flattered and overwhelmed. Yet at the same time she found herself thinking once more that Jim Holbrook certainly liked to have things his way. She couldn't say she wasn't enjoying going along with him. On the other hand, she mused idly, in the real world, that might lead to the same kind of trouble she'd had with Bruce—she'd never been the type who liked to be managed.

Terri looked around at the idyllic scene. This wasn't the real world, she reminded herself. It was a thoroughly enjoyable fantasy, and Jim Holbrook was doing his utmost to make it magical for her.

As he leaned over the basket, a jar of salmon pâté emerged, followed by a loaf of crusty French bread and a container each of green grapes and fresh raspberries. While Terri continued to watch, wide-eyed, Jim followed that with a variety of spreads and cheeses, half a roast chicken, and slices of four different kinds of luscious-looking pastry.

"This isn't lunch. It's a full-blown Roman banquet," she commented as she finally sat down beside him. "Don't tell me *you* know as much about gourmet food as I do."

"Probably not. But when you live alone, you like to indulge yourself sometimes." He cut off a slice of French bread, spread it with pâté and handed it to her.

While she munched on it appreciatively, Jim brought out china plates, snowy white cloth napkins and gleaming cutlery from the bottom of the basket. Terri was past being surprised. Instead, she surreptitiously studied the man who had arranged this intimate picnic in the woods. He was sitting on the other side of the blanket, expertly uncorking the bottle of sauvignon blanc. Watching his powerful hands, she suddenly remembered how they'd felt on her body last night.

As though he sensed her gaze on him, he looked up. Again she had the disturbing feeling that he was reading her mind.

The need to break the sudden tension between them with conversation became palpable, and she blurted out the first question that came into her head. "Have you always been a bachelor, Jim?"

"No," he admitted. He poured the white wine into two long-stemmed glasses and handed her one. "I'm a widower, actually."

"Oh, I'm sorry."

"Don't be. It happened a long time ago. I hardly remember what living with someone was like. How about you? Have you always been single?"

Terri nodded. "I was engaged in college, but it didn't work out. Since then I've just been too busy to have much social life."

"Well, I'm glad I caught you on vacation."

It wasn't exactly a vacation, but instead of starting in on that, Terri decided to bring the conversation back to the food.

"These raspberries are absolutely delicious—and decadent."

Smoothly, Jim picked up her cue. "Mmm-hmm. I was amazed when the hotel said they were available. Do they get them from Spain, do you suppose?"

Terri laughed at him. "I thought you were the one who knew so much about local flora. Some varieties of raspberries have two seasons. This has to be the end of the late crop."

"Touché," he said, raising the wine bottle and filling her glass. "You see, we have things to teach each other."

Terri watched the pale liquid rise to the rim. "Yes, I guess we do. You have nothing to learn about wine, though. This is wonderful, only I'm not sure it's such a good idea for me to drink any more of it. Wine in the middle of the day always makes me sleepy."

"But you're on a holiday. You can sneak a nap after lunch if you want."

"That's right. I can," Terri admitted, taking another sip. "But is it really safe to sleep out here in the woods?"

"I'll watch over you."

Terri's gaze drifted over him. He had propped his back against a tree and was sitting with his long legs crossed comfortably at the ankles. Again she had that sensation of familiarity, as if they'd known each other for a long time. Yet, here in the solitude of the woods, her feeling of comfort with him was spiced with sexual awareness. And all her instincts told her that the same was true for him.

"What are you thinking now?" he asked lazily.

Terri glanced away. "Just enjoying the wine and the company," she half fibbed. That was true as far as it went, she told herself. "I'd like to hear more of your Boy Scout adventures."

Jim laughed. "You want me to tell you how I learned to recognize poison ivy? It was when we dug the latrine in a patch of the stuff."

When they had finished laughing together, Terri said, "So you were holding out on me."

"Well, I wasn't going to trust you with *that* until I knew you better. You look as though you need something to lean against,'' he added. ''Why don't you come over here, and we can share this tree trunk.''

In truth, Terri's back was beginning to reproach her for trying to eat while reclining on the ground. Yet despite the closeness that had been developing between them, she hesitated to accept his invitation.

Jim caught the conflicting emotions that were reflected on her face. ''I didn't bring you out here with the idea of a woodland seduction,'' he assured her.

''How can I be sure of that?'' she challenged him playfully.

''By coming over here and letting me prove it.''

It was impossible for Terri not to respond to the flicker of provocative amusement in his dark eyes. Gracefully she got up. Bringing her plate and wineglass, she came around to the other corner of the blanket. Had she imagined that flash of triumph in Jim's smile? she wondered.

He moved to one side so that there was room to settle next to him. ''See? Now isn't that much more comfortable?'' he asked when she'd arranged herself against the tree.

''Mmm.'' Actually, it was in one way, but not in another. Now, with his shoulder pressed against hers and his thigh half an inch away, she felt more under his spell than ever.

Her hand trembled slightly, and to cover the outward display of nerves, she reached quickly for a bit of cheese on her plate. But her unsteady fingers brushed against the wineglass, and it tipped, spilling the contents on her pant leg.

''Oh!'' she exclaimed.

''Let me get that.'' Jim reached for a napkin and pressed it against the wet fabric covering her lower leg. She sucked in her breath suddenly as she felt the impact of each of his fingers through her jeans.

He sensed the reaction and misinterpreted its cause. ''That clammy material can't feel very good against your skin.'' Before she realized what he was going to do, he slipped his free hand under the cuff and up along her calf so that he could hold the wet denim away from her. While his warm palm rested against her flesh, he worked to blot up the spill. Terri stared down at what he was doing, but all of her awareness was focused on the few square inches held captive by his warm hand. Little rivulets of excitement seemed to flow up her leg. If she could have moved without looking like a fool, she would have jerked away.

"You don't have to do that." To her own ears her voice sounded breathless.

"But I want to. I didn't bring you out here to make you uncomfortable," Jim said, dabbing up the last of the moisture. As he spoke, he rubbed his thumb gently back and forth along the swell of her leg. It was impossible for Terri not to give in to the sensation. Closing her eyes, she leaned back against him.

It was an unpleasant shock when he withdrew the heat of his hand from her sensitized skin, and her eyes flew open.

"All fixed," he said, carefully smoothing her pant leg around her ankle. "And I know just what you need now."

"What?" Terri struggled to breathe. Did he know how erotically his touch had affected her? And was he feeling the same thing? In fact, had he done it deliberately? She risked a sidewise glance, but his expression didn't give her any clue.

"Something sweet will take your mind off your troubles." As though seduction were the furthest thing from his mind, Jim reached out and brought over the plate with the desserts.

"Those look sinfully delicious," Terri declared, hearing the sultry note in her voice and lowering her lashes.

"Don't they, though," he agreed. "What's your pleasure? We have double chocolate cake with fudge icing, rum torte, apricot tart glacé, and mocha mint cheesecake."

"Does anybody leave this place weighing less than three hundred pounds?"

"If you're worried, we can schedule a heavy session in the gym. And I hear they have a roller rink where you can work off some more calories."

"Even if we do both those things—can we possibly eat all this?"

"Let's start small and work our way up," he said. For a moment Jim's gaze caressed her, and she warmed to it just as surely as if he still held her in his grasp. Then he looked down and began neatly dividing each of the pastries into quarters.

Terri forced herself to concentrate on the sweets.

"What do you want?" he asked huskily.

Instead of telling him, Terri stared helplessly into his eyes. She slid the edge of her tongue along her lips and watched as his gaze followed the movement.

"Then let me decide for you. Chocolate has always been one of my favorites." Between his strong thumb and forefinger he picked up a piece of the rich double fudge cake and held it out toward her. She didn't move. Eyes locked with hers, he raised the confection to her lips. Succumbing hypnotically to this lesser temptation, Terri took a bite.

"How is it?"

"Delicious," she murmured as it melted sensuously on her tongue.

"Then I'd better try it, too."

She watched as he brought the cake to his own mouth and had some. "It is delicious," he agreed in his deep baritone. "But the best part is knowing you've already tasted it." As if opening the gate to forbidden delights, he silently lifted the plate and offered it to her.

Unable to find words to respond to his provocative remark, Terri reached for another sweet.

"Turnabout is fair play, you know," Jim said.

"What?" Seeing the glint in his eyes and understanding his meaning, she extended her fingers and offered him the piece of apricot tart.

Jim leaned forward and took a bite. Then, with the taste of apricot still on his lips, he pulled Terri into his arms and kissed her.

"This is a lot better than dessert," he growled.

"Yes," she agreed, her arms going up around his neck as she opened her lips eagerly under Jim's. Unable to resist the invitation, he deepened the kiss, stroking the silky interior of her mouth with his tongue. He bent her backward, and Terri moaned as he caressed first the underside of her chin and then her throat.

"Oh, Terri," he groaned. She was so soft, so pliant and desirable in his arms. He slid his lips down to the soft V between her breasts where the top button of her blouse had come open. To his delight, she arched into the caress. Turning his face from side to side, he dropped fevered kisses along the mounded flesh at the edge of her demibra. She was yielding to him eagerly. At the realization, he dropped his hand to the snap at the waistband of her jeans. The need to feel her naked beneath him was almost as real as the need to draw breath into his lungs.

Then he clenched his hand and his whole body grew rigid with the effort to make himself stop. It was bad enough that he had to deceive her about his identity. No way would he break a promise he'd made to her—no matter how much it cost him.

"What is it?" she asked.

Terri's voice was high and reedy. The emotion quivering in it almost made him drag his lips back to hers.

"I can't." With a sigh he lifted his head and put his hands on her shoulders, creating several inches of space between the two of them. With a dazed expression in her eyes, she stared at him uncomprehendingly, suddenly chilled by the withdrawal of his body heat.

"I did promise, didn't I?" he said regretfully.

"Promise what?"

"To be a gentleman." With fingers that felt thick and clumsy he rebuttoned her blouse. "But we'd better not stay out here any longer if I'm going to keep my Boy Scout's word of honor."

Five

―――

There weren't many men who wouldn't have taken advantage of a willing woman in the woods, Terri mused as she and Jim headed back toward the hotel. She glanced in his direction. He really was a man of his word. Unfortunately, she wasn't so sure she was glad of that. Under her rebuttoned blouse, her breasts still tingled from the touch of his mouth, and her body was taut with frustration. Back by the waterfall, she had been completely caught up in the erotic sensations of the moment. She knew very well what would have happened if Jim hadn't drawn back.

Suddenly she could no longer ignore an image of herself pinned beneath his powerful body—the silent trees their only audience, the sky their only roof.

She shivered at the very thought.

"Something wrong?" Jim asked.

"Nothing." The question had taken her by surprise. He, too, had seemed caught up in his own private thoughts. Yet obviously he was just as attuned to her as she to him.

"Are you sure you're not cold?"

"No, really. I'm just fine."

Jim glanced down at the top of her slightly tousled dark head. From the quaver in her voice, he suspected that she wasn't telling the truth. But he wasn't about to contradict her right now. He was dealing with problems of his own. Terri could have no idea what it had cost him to lift his head from her breasts and set her body away from his.

There had been several flustered moments during which they had busied themselves cleaning up the picnic debris. Terri had offered to carry the blanket back to the hotel, but he'd gallantly refused. In fact, their picnic cloth was the perfect cover for his present very visible discomfort. With one arm bent he held the blanket in front of him like a shield while he hefted the picnic basket with the other hand.

Smiling wryly at himself, Jim shook his head. He couldn't remember another occasion when keeping his word had been quite so painful. What he needed, he decided, was a plunge into a pool of ice-cold water. But he'd have to settle for a nippy shower in the privacy of his room. After that, perhaps he could work off some of his excess energy in the Hearthwood fitness center.

"So, are we going to try the exercise facilities even if we didn't get much dessert?" he asked Terri.

She nodded, thinking that she had come very close to being dessert herself.

"Good, I'll meet you there in a half hour."

"I might not be down quite so soon," Terri said as they waited for the elevator. She was thinking that she might need a little more time to compose herself, although she wasn't going to admit that to Jim. He seemed to have easily thrown off the erotic mood that had possessed them both a few minutes earlier.

"Take your time. I can always get started by myself."

Up in her room, she dawdled in a warm shower and then debated whether to wear her burgundy and blue shorts and top or her lavender leotard. Finally she settled on the former as being a bit more conservative. Although why, after last night and this afternoon, she should think that was necessary, she didn't know.

By the time she'd packed her suit and a towel and arrived at the weight room, she was at least twenty minutes late. She hovered outside the floor-to-ceiling glass windows that enclosed the entrance to the facility. Since fewer than half a dozen people were using the equipment, it was easy to spot Jim on the far side of the room. He wasn't alone, however. Terri frowned.

Dressed in sweatpants and a T-shirt, he was lying on an exercise bench. Leaning over him with her breasts almost in his face was a lithe blonde, who sported leotards cut so high that they practically scraped her armpits. Terri glanced down at her own sober little outfit and suddenly regretted her choice of attire. She lifted her head from her rueful inspection, to see Jim grinning up engagingly at the young woman. A bolt of pure jealousy shot through Terri. Encouraged by his smile, the blonde put her hand on Jim's thigh and squeezed. That was just too much for Terri, and she pushed open the glass door. But as she strode across the room toward the objects of her scrutiny, she wondered what she was going to say. She had just met Jim Holbrook yesterday and couldn't exactly claim that he was her private property.

"You must work out at home," the blonde was burbling as she ran her fingers up and down the side of his chest. "There's not an ounce of fat on you. Your serratus magnus feels terrific. And your external oblique is all right, too. Much more impressive than mine," she added, picking up his hand and laying his palm just under her jutting breasts.

"I think he can take care of his own external oblique," Terri heard herself interject.

The blonde's head snapped around. Jim followed her gaze with leisurely amusement. But he saw that Terri was too caught up in her confrontation with the female exercise teacher to notice his expression.

"Oh, you must be Mrs. Holbrook. Let me introduce myself," she said, sticking out a muscular hand. "I'm Wendy, the pro on duty this afternoon. I was just setting your husband up with the proper equipment."

As the woman spoke, Terri's eyes met the unholy twinkle in Jim's. She had to bite her tongue to keep from blurting out, *He's already got the proper equipment.*

Wendy cast a critical glance over Terri's upper body. "You, on the other hand, could use some work on those triceps."

"I don't know," Jim commented with a maddeningly straight face. "Her triceps feel pretty good to me."

"I believe triceps are in the arms," Terri informed him. That was not where his eyes had been lingering.

Wendy looked from one to the other, obviously rather nonplussed at the byplay. "Perhaps the two of you would like to try the exercise bikes. We have a special model with a heart monitor." Without waiting to see if they were following, she started across the room.

"That sounds interesting," Jim agreed, sitting up. For the first time Terri saw the legend on his T-shirt. It said, Never Play Leapfrog with a Unicorn.

"Where did you run across that?"

"A present from my secretary."

"Oh."

He let that sink in before adding, "She's the motherly type. But she's got a sense of humor." He'd been presented with the shirt after a particularly harrowing round of business negotiations regarding the opening of the Sommerset Mall. His face flushed as he was reminded of his business connection with Terri.

"Too hard a workout?" Terri asked anxiously.

"No. I'm okay. Let's not keep Tinker Bell's friend waiting."

Terri laughed but couldn't help wondering why he'd had that odd expression on his face. What had he been thinking of? she mused as she lengthened her stride to follow him to where Wendy stood waiting with hands on hips.

"We've only got one monitor," the curvaceous instructor informed them. "Which one of you wants to use it?"

Not sure what was involved, Terri was about to decline when Jim spoke up. "Let Terri have a chance. I've got one at home."

Wendy picked up a small metal clip attached to a plastic-covered wire. "Let me put this to your earlobe, then."

Terri nodded. She'd been half afraid that they were going to tape it to her chest. As soon as the device came into contact with her skin, a small transmitter on the bike began to beep.

"The readout is over here," Wendy informed her, pointing to a small screen at the top of the handlebars that registered sixty-one.

"Your resting heart rate is very good," Jim commented, leaning over to look. As he moved close to her and put his hand on her shoulder, the beeping accelerated and the number went up to seventy-eight. He grinned. "Hmm, I hadn't realized what an interesting little gizmo this really is."

Ignoring him, Terri climbed on the bike. "I'm just nervous about having an audience," she mumbled.

"Oh, don't be," Wendy soothed her. "Let me explain it to you. The readout shows your apparent heart rate per minute, although it changes constantly. I'd guess you want to shoot for an exercising rate of about one hundred and thirty-five."

"Then I'd better get pedaling," Terri muttered.

After she'd checked the tension on the machine, the blonde finally went away and left them alone. Jim climbed on the bike beside hers and they both pedaled in silence. Terri kept the speedometer at a steady twenty miles an hour and watched her heart rate climb.

She was soon tired, and uncomfortably aware of the bike seat's sharp edge against her inner thighs. If Jim hadn't been there, she would have quit. But he was pedaling along effortlessly beside her, and she was embarrassed to be shown up so easily.

After a few minutes, she noticed he was glancing over at her monitor. The readout had climbed to over one hundred forty-five.

"Is that good or bad?" she asked.

"It's not bad, but I suspect it means you're not used to this much exertion."

Terri frowned. Between him and Wendy, she was beginning to feel like a little old lady. For a few moments more she pedaled on in an irritated silence, then stopped.

The rhythm of the monitor slowed almost at once.

"See how fast you get back to normal," Jim observed.

"What am I looking for, exactly?"

"The quicker you return to your resting heart rate, the better."

"Obviously you do a lot of this sort of thing."

"I stop by the health club three or four times a week."

"And do you find it as easy to pick up adoring blondes at your regular club as you did here?"

Jim studied her, looking not at all displeased. "The answer is no. I'm on too tight a schedule to do anything but work out."

"You mean there aren't any Wendy birds hanging around the weight room?"

"Yes," he admitted, his smile widening. "There are a few. But none of them is my type."

"And what is your type?"

"Until a few hours ago, I didn't know I had one. But now I've decided it's classy brunettes."

Terri couldn't help smiling. "Even if they don't have the approved pulse rate?"

"Oh, I believe I can think of a remedy for that." Jim got off his bike and ran his thumb along the edge of her ear. At his touch, the monitor, which had been beeping along at a slow, steady rate, suddenly began to clatter. Smiling even more broadly, he gently unfastened the clip. "See what I mean?" he whispered in her ear.

"That's cheating."

"I'm not above cheating a little bit to get what I want."

While Terri was still digesting that information, he went on. "Now that we know your heart can take it, why don't we find out what else Hearthwood has to offer?"

"All right," Terri agreed. "Lead the way."

In fact, except for the few hours when they slept in their own rooms, Terri and Jim spent almost all of the next twenty-four hours together. Jim took her for a canoe ride on the lake, and afterward they enjoyed cocktails on the terrace, where they talked more about their favorite movies—and books. Again, Terri was struck by how much she and Jim had in common. Even though their childhoods couldn't have been more different, their interests and attitudes meshed closely. But underneath the animated conversation, she was still conscious of the sexual currents flowing between them.

Although Terri was half hoping for something more, they parted after dinner with only a light kiss and a promise to meet the next morning again. Terri stood outside her door, regretfully watching Jim's retreating shoulders.

She woke up Sunday morning feeling a sense of loss that she couldn't understand at first. Then she realized what it was. This was going to be her last day at Hearthwood with Jim. For all she knew, she'd never see him again.

It must have been on his mind, too. After they'd gotten their breakfast, he looked across at her. "This is our last day."

Terri's heart started to thump.

"But it's not really the last, because we're going to go on seeing each other after we get back home, aren't we?" he questioned.

Terri nodded. She hadn't wanted it to end either, but somehow she couldn't have spoken first and told Jim how she felt. Now that he'd done it for her, she felt as if a lead weight had been lifted off her chest.

He must have caught the expression on her face. "I'm glad you feel the same way," he murmured with a smile. Then his manner became purposeful. "But since it's our last day in this paradise, let's make the most of it."

Following breakfast, they played croquet and tried one of the other walking trails that led to a spectacular mountain overlook. Then, after a leisurely lunch, Jim got out one of the Hearthwood brochures. "You know what? They've got a new roller rink here."

Terri looked at him uncertainly. "I did skate when I was a kid. But my experience is strictly of the sidewalk variety."

"That means we'll be holding each other up," Jim said, putting his arm around her shoulder. "I don't mind if you don't. And maybe afterward we can soothe our aching bodies in the heated pool. In fact, why don't we bring along our suits?"

Terri agreed, and they met twenty minutes later at the roller rink's rental desk. She'd never worn shoe skates before and allowed Jim to lace them up. After he'd donned his own, he grinned and held out his hands. In a moment, they were slowly making their way across the carpet to the rink.

She and Jim must look like a comedy team to the other people in the rink, Terri decided. Between gales of laughter, they both took several pratfalls. And once, another skater almost fell over them. But through it all, Jim remained good-humored. He really was an amazing person, Terri thought. Most men were far too concerned about their dignity to risk looking ridiculous. But Jim radiated such confidence in his masculinity that clowning around on roller skates left him unfazed. Besides, once he got his balance back, she could see that he must have been very good at this as a kid. He could even skate backward, something she'd always wanted to learn to do.

"We make a great pair. Maybe we should go out for the Olympics," Jim joked as he spun Terri around, all the while holding her firmly with his strong hands. In his arms like this, she felt a strange mixture of excitement, coupled with a certainty that he would never let her fall.

"I think they only have ice skating in the Olympics, not roller skating," Terri pointed out breathlessly. "And anyway, I don't have the feet for it. I think I'm getting blisters."

"Then it's time you slipped into some nice, warm water. How about heading for the pool now? I'll meet you outside the ladies' locker room."

A few minutes later, Terri was standing in the hall, wearing a royal-blue maillot under her robe. She was looking out the window at the mountains when Jim came up behind her and put his hand on her shoulder.

"All ready?" he asked.

She turned. He was dressed in a nubby white robe that was a perfect foil for the healthy tan of his skin. Below it, Terri caught a glimpse of muscular, hair-dusted legs. Suddenly she realized that she was about to experience the pleasure of seeing him all but undressed.

He caught the expression on her face. "You're smiling. What are you thinking about?"

"Oh, I was just wondering what that grotto is really like," she said airily.

"Well, then, let's go find out. I'm anxious to see it myself." He took her hand, and they moved toward a red-carpeted stairway that led to the lower floor.

Once downstairs, they walked along a corridor where they could hear the hollow echo of voices and splashing water. A large sign directing them to the left was decorated with pictures of mermaids wearing nothing but seashell bras and sea anemone necklaces.

"Someone around here certainly has a vivid imagination," Terri murmured.

"Well, let's see if the place lives up to its advance billing," Jim suggested, pulling open a polished mahogany door with a brass sea horse for a handle. As they stepped into the room, they were enveloped by a gust of warm, moist flower-scented air. In the background, the gentle strains of a Hawaiian love song wafted through the speakers of a high-fidelity sound system. But the visual aspects of the grotto were by far the most striking.

Terri looked around in wonder, feeling as if she'd stumbled into an underground paradise. Before them an irregularly shaped pool of crystal-clear water beckoned. It was entirely enclosed by what looked like the inside of a mountain illuminated with blue and violet light. Down one side cascaded a gentle waterfall flanked by ferns and orchids. Leading off to the sides were partially submerged tunnels. The whole effect was of a lush, intimate adult playground.

"I can't believe this place!" Jim exclaimed.

"It's fantastic," Terri agreed. "What do you suppose those are?" She pointed to the tunnels.

"I expect we're going to find out," Jim answered. "My guess is that it's going to be fun exploring."

As they watched, a smiling couple holding hands emerged from one of the passages.

"Well, whatever they were doing, it looks as if they were having a good time," Jim commented.

Terri had approached the edge of the pool and dipped her toe into the water.

"It's warm as a bath."

"I can imagine coming off the ski slopes in winter and escaping down here is quite a treat," Jim murmured as he untied his robe. She watched as he casually shrugged out of

the garment and folded it on one of the benches that had
been molded into the rock-simulating walls.

With her eyes riveted on his back, Terri's fingers froze on
the belt of her own robe. At the sight of Jim in his black
bathing trunks, she drew in a quick breath. She had secretly been picturing how he would look without clothes.
Now she realized that her imagination hadn't come anywhere near the reality of his magnificent near nudity.

His back was broad and muscled. Below his lean waist,
his buttocks were firm and tantalizingly rounded. When he
turned, the view from the front was even better. Like his
back, his chest was broad and muscular, but it was covered
with a thick mat of hair that was several shades lighter than
what she had expected. It tapered downward dramatically,
leading her eyes to a flat belly that she somehow knew was
rock-hard. Below that were lean and dangerous hips that
even the conservative cut of his bathing suit could not dis-
guise. Realizing that she was staring, Terri wrenched her
gaze away. In one swift gesture, she finished taking off her
own robe.

She knew Jim was looking at her, just as she had at him.
And as she walked across the pebble-textured floor and laid
her cover-up over his, she felt her breath wedge in her
throat. She wanted to say something to break the tension of
the moment; instead, she twisted her fingers in the soft fabric of the robe. The surface of her flesh seemed to tingle
where his eyes lingered.

''Turn around and let me look at you.'' His voice was
gruff.

She wanted to refuse, but she simply straightened and
pivoted, meeting his eyes a little defiantly. It had been a long
time since she had given much thought to how she looked in
a bathing suit. Now she felt acutely self-conscious about her
bare white skin and wished she'd had the time to acquire a
tan this summer. What did Jim think of her pale complex-

ion? she wondered. Were her hips too wide for his taste? Were her thighs firm enough?

"You look like an ivory statue," he murmured.

"I—"

"But we both know you're much warmer than ivory," Jim said thickly. She held her breath as he reached out and ran his finger down her bare arm. In response, the tiny hairs on the surface of her skin stood straight up, and she shivered. "You know, don't you, that that modest little suit makes you look sexy as hell," he said in a husky voice.

She couldn't think of an answer, and he didn't wait for one.

"I think I'd better take that dip right away," he said. He strode to the edge of the pool, sliced the water with a clean dive and disappeared below the azure surface.

Terri stood at the side of the pool, looking at the concentric ripples. She'd never met a man who could be so openly sensual. Perhaps that was one of the things that attracted her to him—the honesty of his approach to life.

It was very different from the games most men played. Suddenly she acknowledged to herself that she wanted to learn what he had to teach her.

With new boldness, she approached the side of the pool. There were other couples in the water, but as far as she was concerned, the pool might have been empty except for Jim Holbrook. He was under the water for much longer than she could ever have held her breath. At last he resurfaced and threw back his head, water streaming off his dark hair. With slow, easy movements, he stroked to the edge, rested his elbows on the side and looked up at Terri.

"Come on in."

"I'm not that good a swimmer."

"Then I'll keep you afloat." He raised his hand to take hers. Obediently, Terri sat down on the edge and eased herself in. The water sliding up her body and covering her shoulders was pleasantly warm. But she was much more conscious of Jim's strong hands as they closed around her waist and supported it.

"I really should have gotten in at the shallow end," she protested.

"Oh, no. This is much more fun. How well do you swim?"

"Well enough to pass the high school test. But only just."

"Did the test include floating?"

"A little."

One of his hands moved down to her hips, while the other wrapped gently around the back of her neck. "Let's see if you can still do it."

While she gazed up at his face, he tipped her up in the water and stretched her out on its cushiony surface, one arm under her shoulders and the other under her hips.

"Good. That's very good."

A wave splashed against her face, and she tensed. He moved so that his chest shielded her. "Just relax and let me do all the work. I'm going to float you down to the shallow end."

Terri closed her eyes, enjoying the feeling of his strong hands on her body. His torso was inches from her face, and she had to stifle the impulse to turn her head to the side and press her lips against his firm, wet skin. Once again he was taking charge. In this warm, watery environment, it was quite enjoyable. Would he be this way in bed? she wondered, and then felt her skin grow hot. Suddenly she struggled to right herself.

"Easy," he said as her arms and legs tangled with his. "You were doing so well. What made you go stiff on me that way?" he asked, then pulled her against him and slid her slowly down the length of his water-slick body. It seemed hours before her feet finally touched the pool's sloping bottom.

She could have stepped back. But for a long moment she stood with her soft curves pressed to his hard planes, acknowledging silently that she'd been longing to do this since that first night in front of the television set. As her hands rested lightly on his shoulders, she felt a ripple of reaction tauten his muscles. Her own body had tightened with a rising excitement, and her thighs suddenly felt weak and warm.

"This dip isn't exactly cooling me off the way I anticipated," Jim growled in her ear.

Terri took a step backward. "Maybe we should explore those caves," she suggested breathily.

"That's a good idea." Threading his fingers between hers, he led her through the warm, shallow water to the nearest entrance. As they stepped under the rocky overhang, she realized that they had entered an intimate hideaway that created an illusion of almost total privacy. Immediately the sounds of the other swimmers died away to faint echoes.

Terri hadn't been quite prepared for such seclusion. When Jim began to wrap his arms around her waist, she tugged herself free from his grasp and crossed over to the large saltwater aquarium set in the wall. Inside, brilliantly colored fish swam lazily in and out of what looked like a coral reef.

"They've thought of almost everything, haven't they?"

"Mmm. Are you into tropical fish?" Jim had come up behind her.

"I don't collect them. But I've always thought it would be fun, because they're so beautiful." She focused on a graceful blue angel. But as Jim drew her close and nibbled his way up her neck toward her ear, she closed her eyes.

"You aren't interested in the fish at all, are you?" she accused him in a throaty little gasp.

"Nope. You're the only one who interests me right now."

She might have been boneless as he drew her back through the warm, thigh-high water toward the heat of his body. As the skin of her lower back brushed the taut muscles of his stomach, she realized that his flesh was giving off more heat than the water. But so was hers, she acknowledged.

"This really is paradise," Jim whispered between tiny kisses that made her nerve endings tingle.

As his mouth teased her neck and the tender coil of her ear, he outlined the curves of her body with his hands, sliding them sensuously from her narrow rib cage to her tiny waist. After a moment they moved downward, as though taking in the feminine roundness of her hips. Then, as his hands settled possessively on the span of her pelvic bones, he groaned and pulled her closer still.

A little gasp escaped her lips as she became blazingly aware of his arousal. She slumped back against him. If he hadn't been holding her up, she would have slipped into the water.

His lips were against her ear, and he spoke in low, urgent tones. "What's been going on between us has been like a movie on fast forward, you know. We might have met only two days ago, but a lot has happened in a very short time. Do you believe that?"

Her throat was so constricted that she couldn't answer.

"Do you?" he prompted more urgently.

"Yes," she managed to whisper.

"Why do you think I've been trying to keep the two of us busy with every sport known to man? Why do you think I haven't initiated anything like this since that first night?" he asked.

Terri was unable to respond.

"Because I promised myself that I wouldn't—until we got back to reality. But now I simply can't help myself."

With that he swung her around so that she was facing him. For several heartbeats he gazed down into her face, taking in the flushed cheeks, quickening breath and pupils dilated with passion. Then he drew her close to him, once more imprinting her with the hard evidence of his need. Almost roughly he tipped her head back and covered her mouth with his.

She hadn't realized before how much he'd been holding himself back—even on the night they'd met. Now, for the first time, she felt the full impact of his male demand. It triggered her own desire. Suddenly overflowing with the compulsion to give him what he was demanding, Terri returned the kiss with every bit of strength in her.

As his mouth plundered hers, his hands ranged hungrily over her body, scooping out the hollow of her waist, stroking the roundness of her bottom, teasing the sides of her breasts so that her nipples begged for his touch.

When Jim and Terri finally broke apart, both were trembling.

"What if someone walks in here?" Terri gasped.

She felt the vibration of a laugh deep in his chest. "We can close our eyes."

"You can't mean that."

"You're right," he agreed, his voice a low growl in the warm shelter of the cave. "I think the way to solve the problem is to go up to my room."

"Yes." The strength of her resolve surprised her. She could no more deny him or herself than change into a butterfly and flit out of his grasp.

Their arms wrapped around each other's waist, they made their way toward the edge of the pool. Although they were both in a hurry, the resistance of the thigh-high water held them back. It felt almost as though they were struggling through some primeval element. There might have been other swimmers in the pool, but neither Jim nor Terri saw anyone else.

When they reached the side, Jim lifted Terri and set her on the cement. Instead of following, he stood with the blue water swirling around his waist, looking up at her quizzically.

"Aren't you coming out?" she questioned.

Jim glanced around, suddenly aware that they weren't really alone. "I think you'd better bring my robe over before I climb up there."

"Oh!" She felt the blood rush to her cheeks as she realized what he meant. Yet at the same time, the knowledge that he was in such straits only heightened her excitement.

After Terri and Jim were wrapped in their robes, he threaded his fingers through hers and led her back to the entrance.

When he opened the door, they were hit by a wall of cool air. As it washed over Terri's skin, she looked up uncertainly at Jim. There was a very private sort of look on his face—a taut intensity that one didn't normally display in public. She could imagine that the same sort of expression molded her features. Could they both walk up the stairs and to the elevators like this? she asked herself. Surely they would give themselves away to anyone who happened to glance in their direction!

Normally that would have been enough to make her reconsider. But not now. Now she was willing to walk through fire to be alone with Jim where they could express the feelings that threatened to overpower them.

Six

I've been wanting this since the first moment I saw you."

"Yes."

Jim leaned back against the closed door of his room, drawing her tightly against his body. To their mutual frustration, the contact was cushioned by layers of thick terry cloth. Impatiently he fumbled at the tie of his robe. Terri worked at her own. But excitement had made her fingers so clumsy that she could barely manage the simple knot.

It seemed like an eternity before the robes were pooled on the carpet around their feet. Then once again Jim was pulling her back into his arms. For a few moments he simply held her, luxuriating in the feeling of her scantily clad body pressed against his, but there was still too much between them to satisfy him for long. Soon he began to tug at the straps of her damp bathing suit. Terri swayed slightly on her feet. She was incapable of movement while he maneuvered her arms out of the top of the suit.

"This is like a second skin on you," he rumbled, "but I'd rather have the real thing." As he spoke, he peeled the slick, stretchy material down almost to her hips.

She heard him draw in a sharp breath as he devoured her with his eyes. Looking up, she caught his fevered expression. It was so intense that she began to quiver all over. Then he was bending her backward so that he could kiss her breasts. Instinctively she closed her eyes and reached out to steady her hands against his broad shoulders.

Her flesh was still cool from the damp suit, and the tips of her breasts were already erect. The furnace of Jim's mouth was an instant antidote to the chill, yet it only made her nipples more taut.

As his tongue swirled around them, a little sob escaped Terri's lips.

"Do you like that, my love?"

She couldn't speak, but dug her fingers into his hard muscles as she gave herself up to the heady pleasure of his caresses.

From her breasts his mouth moved down the soft slope of her torso to the gentle curve of her belly. Kneeling before her, he once more hooked his thumbs in the top of the damp suit and slowly pulled it down over her thighs and legs.

As he rubbed his cheek against the soft skin of her hip, Terri felt his breath warming and stirring her most secret and responsive places.

When he felt her body stiffen, he hesitated for a moment. He'd guessed she wasn't very experienced. All at once he was glad, even if it meant she wasn't quite ready for the depth of the intimacy he craved. But she would be, he thought. He held her still for one final searing kiss against the soft curve of her belly. Then he stood up and looked intensely at her.

Terri nodded fractionally in answer to his unspoken question.

An instant later she was in his arms, cradled against his heart, and he was striding across the room.

After stripping back the spread, he laid her gently on the cool sheets. Then, impatiently, he struggled to peel off his own suit. Terri reached toward him, and he was beside her on the bed, enfolding her in his arms, kissing her deeply. Desire, hot and electric, throbbed palpably between them.

Terri twined her legs with Jim's. She was always such a controlled person, but being with Jim had robbed her of the ability to chain her passions—passions she hadn't even known existed. Never in her life had she been so aroused.

A pleading sob escaped from her lips. It was as though she were burning up from the inside out and would go up in flames if Jim didn't put out the fire.

"Easy, sweetheart," he cautioned. "If you keep that up, it's going to be all over before it really gets started. And I want you to need me just as badly as I need you."

"I do!" she gasped.

Drawing back slightly, he crooked a not quite steady finger under her chin and tipped her face up to his. She stared at him imploringly. His eyes held a mixture of passion and seriousness that made something in the pit of her stomach contract. She couldn't imagine wanting him any more than she did at this moment. Her blood was boiling, melting her very core.

He might have intended to prolong their foreplay. But it was impossible for him to hold back, just as it was for her. With a groan he lowered his mouth to hers again, drinking in her sweetness while his hands stroked the hot center of her desire. The caresses brought them both to flash point. Suddenly it wasn't possible for either of them to wait any longer.

Frantically Terri urged him toward her, clasping his narrow hips between her thighs. With satisfaction she felt the hard, probing pressure of his masculinity against her aching softness. He entered her in a sure, powerful thrust that made her gasp.

"Sweetheart, am I hurting you?" he questioned, struggling to hold himself still above her.

"Just a little bit—at first," she stammered.

"Do you want me to stop?" he asked, his breathing ragged.

"No!" If he left her now, she would die. Clasping her hands around his waist, she laced her fingers together so that she could hold him to her.

But he didn't need to be persuaded. When he looked down into the shimmering emerald pools of her eyes, he was trapped in their depths—just as his body was a prisoner of gratification deep inside hers. He couldn't have withdrawn from her now if his life depended on it.

Desperately he tried to move slowly, to make his body wait. But his need for satisfaction was too urgent to be restrained for more than a moment or two.

"Please. Jim. Oh, I need—" The words were torn from her lips, even as her nails dug mindlessly into the straining muscles of his hips.

Her passion inflamed his. Together they drove each other toward the edge in a blaze of white heat. His fulfillment triggered hers. As his mouth came down on Terri's, she gave a muffled cry of rapture. Hearts pounding wildly, they clung to each other's damp, trembling bodies.

When Terri finally opened her eyes, she found Jim studying her with an unfathomable expression in his dark eyes.

"Terri, that was—"

"Yes, for me, too," she answered softly.

When he began to shift his weight, she clasped his shoulders. "Don't leave me."

"I'm too heavy." He rolled to the side and took her with him so that as they lay facing each other, their bodies molded together. He smoothed his hands up and down the silky skin of her back.

"You're so lovely, so womanly and so sexy," he added in a low growl.

Terri pressed her face against his shoulder, wondering how to respond to his compliment. She wanted to tell him that he was the sexiest man she had ever met, but the words that came out were "Jim, you're a wonderful lover."

He laughed. "Terri, I suspected that you weren't very experienced. Now I know it."

She was surprised enough to look up into his face. The pleasure of making love with him had been beyond her wildest imaginings. Hadn't she been able to please him? "Why?" she questioned apprehensively.

"Because that was much too fast to be called skillful."

"But—"

He silenced her by nibbling tenderly at her cheek, then tugged gently at her earlobe while he stroked the satin flesh of her thigh.

"You deserve to be loved slowly and tenderly," he whispered. "And now that I'm not so frantic with wanting you, I intend to do just that."

The words were no sooner spoken than he began to kiss and caress her once more. She had thought that her body was sated. But as his hands and mouth warmed and excited her anew, she began to realize that what had gone before had been only a prelude.

"I didn't know..." she murmured on a sob of delight.

"Believe it or not, I didn't know either," he answered, his voice thick with desire.

Soon her body was writhing against Jim's and her hands and lips were caressing him just as eagerly as he was fondling her. But this time he had the strength of purpose to resist her pleas. It wasn't until she was almost out of her mind with unendurable frustration that he joined his body with hers again and drove her beyond the boundaries of ecstasy.

This time they lay in bed for a long time, simply holding each other and savoring the warm contentment that flowed through both of them. The sun had slipped below the horizon when Jim finally stirred.

"You know, we never did have dinner," he murmured into Terri's ear.

"Is that all you think about—eating?"

His rich laughter filled the room. "You can't possibly believe that, can you?"

In the darkness she felt her face grow warm. "I guess not."

"Lunch was a long time ago. And we've expended an awful lot of calories. I can't believe you're not hungry."

After switching on the light, he reached for the room service menu. "We can have anything, from a gourmet dinner to beer and pizza. What's your pleasure?"

Terri gathered the sheet up around her breasts and peered at the list of foods. Suddenly frivolous, she pointed to the ice-cream sundaes. "How about one of those?"

"You must be kidding."

"No. That's really what I'd like."

Jim started to laugh. "Then I guess I'll join you. Only I think I'll order a steak sandwich with my banana split."

Twenty minutes later they sat propped against the pillows, spooning up vanilla ice cream slathered with toppings of hot fudge, strawberry, butterscotch and chopped nuts.

"I haven't done anything like this in years," Jim said as he licked fudge off his spoon. Setting it down, he gave her a direct look. "In fact, it's been years since I've had this good a time."

Terri nodded.

Jim reached over and took Terri's hand. "You know, when we were out there in the woods yesterday, I mentioned that I'd been married before."

"Yes. You said you were a widower."

He hesitated. "It was a happy marriage. But Janet and I were together for only a few years. She was killed by a drunk driver."

"Oh, Jim, how terrible!" Terri exclaimed in sympathy.

"It was a long time ago, and I'm over it. But it changed my life." He paused and cleared his throat. "There are lots of ways to drown your sorrows. I guess I chose to blot out everything else with work. After a while the pain dulled, but by that time I was addicted to my job. And I've been that way ever since."

"I know what you mean," Terri whispered. "There was never any big tragedy in my life. But I guess I had a lot of little dissatisfactions to cope with. Rather than deal with them, I found it easier to throw myself into making my store a success. And now that it's gone, I don't know what I'll do. That's why I got so emotional at breakfast the other morning."

At the mention of Terri's shop, Jim felt a distinct twinge of guilt. It had been two days since he'd learned who she was, and he really should have told her the part he'd inadvertently played in the closing of her business. But the right moment had never presented itself.

He'd told himself he wasn't going to make love to her until he'd been honest with her. But the better he'd gotten to know her, the more he'd wanted her. Finally passion had swept away his good intentions. Now how could he reveal the truth—sitting naked in bed with their empty ice-cream dishes in front of them? And how would she react? He could imagine she might very well feel that he'd deliberately taken advantage of her—though, God knows, there had been nothing in his head except blazing desire when he'd carried her to his bed.

Terri caught the disturbed expression on his face. She clasped her slim fingers around Jim's long, sinewy ones. "Don't worry about me. I've been down. But now I'm feeling as though I can go back and deal with the situation.''

''Maybe there's some way to get T. & H. to reconsider.''
In his mind he was already casting around for something
that would solve her problems without making it look as if
he were paying her for sexual favors.

''Not those skinflints!''

It took every bit of self-control Jim possessed to keep
from flinching. Silently he promised himself that he'd find
a way to tell Terri the truth before they left tomorrow
morning. But not now. ''Let's change the subject,'' he suggested.

Terri was instantly contrite. ''I'm doing it again, aren't
I—letting the real world interfere. I promise I'll stop again.''

''It's not that I can't deal with reality. It's just that I hate
to see you upset—especially now.''

She looked so sweetly kissable, sitting there with the sheet
tucked up around her naked breasts, that he ached to hold
her in his arms again. But a stab of fear intruded on the
tender emotion. He hadn't been lying when he'd told her
how barren his life had been. Even though he'd known Terri
for only a few days, the idea of losing her was unthinkable.

''Terri, you know I want to keep seeing you. So let's make
a pact. Promise me that our relationship won't end when the
weekend is over.''

She gazed into his face, reading the sincere emotion there.
When she'd first met Jim, she certainly hadn't been thinking in terms of anything permanent. And she'd been confused and overwhelmed by the speed at which things
between them had progressed. Just as they had at breakfast, Jim's words made her chest swell with happiness, and
she admitted to herself once again that she couldn't stand
the thought of what they'd found together ending when they
left this place. ''Oh, Jim, of course it won't!'' she cried,
throwing her arms around him. ''I couldn't bear to lose you
either.''

In the next moment they were kissing ardently, all thought of anything but their mutual passion forgotten.

Later that evening Jim sent down to room service again—this time for a bottle of champagne.

"You don't know how close I came to not taking this vacation," he said as he reached over to pour them each a glass of the pale, bubbly wine. Handing one to Terri, he looked into her eyes. Then, slowly and ceremoniously, he clinked his glass with hers. "To new beginnings."

Terri smiled. "To new beginnings, then."

As she lifted the glass to her lips, she again had the sense that she was watching a scene out of a movie. Was she really here, sitting in bed in a luxurious hotel, being toasted by a handsome man who had swept her off her feet, wooed her relentlessly and made love to her with the unbounded passion and finesse of a larger-than-life screen hero? The question made her smile.

"What are you thinking?" Jim asked.

"Oh, I'm just having a hard time believing this is all real."

"Believe it," Jim said, then refilled their glasses.

As they sipped their wine, he leaned back against the pillows and glanced at the clock across the room. It was after midnight.

Terri followed the direction of his gaze.

"We both have a long drive ahead of us in the morning. Maybe we should try to get some sleep."

A little smile quirked his mouth. "We could try, I suppose."

She laughed. They had both been so enraptured with discovering each other that neither had gotten much real rest during the weekend. She knew it was catching up with her. And she suspected that Jim wasn't going to be much good at work the next morning unless he slept. After putting down her glass, she cuddled close to him. "Oh, I bet if you snuggle down under the covers and shut your eyes, you'll drop right off.''

''Think so? If you stay as near to me as this, I wouldn't bet on it.''

''Then I'd better give you a little room.'' She took his glass from his hand, moved over a few inches and switched off the light. But no sooner had she settled down under the covers than he pulled her back against him with a fiercely possessive gesture. ''You're going to think it's silly, but I'm almost afraid to go to sleep.''

The tension in his voice made her look at him with surprise, but she deliberately kept her own words light. ''Don't tell me you're worried about monsters under the bed.''

''Not since I was five. This one is much worse. It's called fear of waking up and finding Terri gone.''

She pressed her cheek against the firm flesh of his shoulder as much to reassure herself as Jim. ''You don't have a thing to worry about. I'm not going anywhere tonight.''

''Then maybe I can close my eyes.''

Beside her, he relaxed. In a few minutes his breathing evened out, and she knew that he'd drifted off. Terri was glad she'd reassured him. Yet she found that the conversation had had the opposite effect on her. Though she closed her own eyes, sleep was impossible, because her mind had begun to churn.

As she tried to find a comfortable position, Terri began to review the weekend—their incredible weekend. Again she had a sense of unreality, as if she simply didn't know the woman who had melted so easily in Jim's arms. She certainly didn't bear much resemblance to the real Terri Genetti—the one who worked long hours, guarded her privacy and was always so cautious about getting into personal relationships.

Terri looked over at Jim, who was sleeping peacefully. Was what they had found together something they could build on, or just a dream born of this fantasy weekend? A dream that would evaporate once they had left this place?

She slid her gaze over Jim's strong profile. How would he respond to the Terri Genetti who got up at precisely seven-thirty every morning and who liked to make her own decisions? And what about his own not very submissive character? It hadn't escaped her that this man liked to be in charge. That hadn't mattered this weekend. But how would it be once they were away from this lush environment where the choices weren't simply between beef Wellington and Maine lobster for dinner?

A frown etched Terri's smooth brow as she restlessly pleated the sheet into folds with her fingers. At her side, Jim murmured something unintelligible. If she kept this up, she was going to wake him. Tenderly she reached out to soothe him, brushing back a strand of dark hair that had fallen across Jim's forehead. Then, regretfully, she eased herself out of the warm bed.

After slipping into Jim's heavy terry cloth robe, she padded to the window. As she tied the belt around her narrow waist, she looked out over the moon-washed lawn and up toward the dark presence of the mountains. She was nervous about what tomorrow would bring, she admitted. For the past few days she been able to forget about the future. But now it was looming before her again. It wasn't just her fears about whether what she and Jim had discovered together would endure. It was everything.

In an unconscious gesture, she slipped her hand into his pocket. Her fingers closed around what she supposed must be his wallet. Perhaps it was safer on the dresser, she thought. But when she went to set it down, she missed the edge of the dresser in the dark and the wallet dropped to the floor and fell open. As she watched in dismay, some cards stuffed into one of the pockets fanned across the floor in front of her.

Terri knelt down to gather them up. One in particular caught her eye, because it was decorated with the T. & H. Management logo. She picked it up and eyed it. Had Jim had some dealings with T. & H. that he hadn't mentioned because she was so down on the company?

At first she couldn't understand what she was seeing. Then she gasped. Jim's name was on the card—along with his title.

She whipped her head around and stared at the bed. The man sleeping so peacefully under the covers was none other than the president of T. & H. Associates.

Terri's heart began to pound, and instantly the throbbing transferred itself to her temples. She told herself to calm down. There had to be some mistake. She must have read it wrong.

Taking a deep, steadying breath, she stood up and carried the card to the window where the moonlight spilled in through the uncurtained panes. Somehow she was hoping against hope that her disturbed thoughts had conjured up the words. Even though her hand trembled, she could still read the legend in front of her eyes: *James Holbrook, President, T. & H. Associates.* The address in nearby Virginia was the company's main office.

Something inside her chest seemed to break, and her vision misted. When she turned to stare back at the bed again, it was through a film of tears. Yet somehow her mind was still functioning. Had Jim read her letter? Her thoughts circled back to the conversations in which she'd mentioned her shop, Sommerset Mall and T. & H. Associates. He hadn't said much. But what he had said had been defensive and evasive, she thought in retrospect. Of course he knew who she was!

She clenched her fist around the card and crumpled it, trying to hold back the sick feeling that threatened to engulf her. All along he had deliberately deceived her. For all she knew, he might have approached her in the lobby out of pure curiosity.

When had he planned to let her know? she wondered. Her first impulse was to stride across the room, yank off his blanket and shake him awake so that she could demand an explanation. Then she realized she didn't want to hear anything he had to say. Right now she felt much too vulnerable for that. She only wanted to get out of that place with what dignity she had left—which wasn't much.

Terri stepped into the bathroom and with cold fingers undid Jim's robe, wadded it up and threw it into the bathtub. Then she yanked her own on. In her haste, she'd somehow mislaid the business card. But that didn't matter. The important thing now was to return to her room, pack and leave. The sooner she got out of there, the sooner she could put the whole sorry incident behind her.

He reached for her in the darkness, and she wasn't there. "Terri?"

There was no answer. A tight knot formed in his chest as he sat up and looked around. In the gray, predawn light, the room looked dismal and colorless. He touched the pillow that still bore the indentation of Terri's head. It was cold, and so were the sheets, which her body should have been warming. Somehow he had known all along that it was going to happen.

Hoping against hope that he was wrong, he looked toward the open bathroom door. Behind it, a square of darkness loomed. He knew she wasn't in there. Nevertheless, he sprang out of bed, strode across the carpet and flicked on the light. Just as he suspected, the little room was deserted. His robe lay in the bathtub as though it had been flung in anger. Something about the way it looked made his blood run cold.

He walked back into the bedroom and glanced around for Terri's bathing suit and robe. They were gone. Sometime during the night she must have dressed and gone back to her room. But she had promised she wouldn't leave. Why had she broken her word?

He glanced across at the phone, then shook his head. He needed to see her face, not just hear her voice.

After stepping into his slacks and shoes, he pulled his shirt on and hastily tucked it into his pants. Then he grabbed his room key and hurried out the door. At this hour the hotel was still quiet and the corridors were deserted. To his dismay, as he approached Terri's door, he saw that it wasn't completely closed.

"Terri?" he called softly. Even as he spoke the words, he knew there was no one in there. He pushed the door open anyway and stepped inside. His gaze flicked to the sofa where they'd sat watching Buck Fielding, unable to think about anything but each other. Quickly he turned away and walked through to the bedroom. The bed looked untouched, and he inhaled sharply when he saw that the closet was empty and the dresser was bare. He knew there was no use checking the bathroom. It was obvious—Terri had packed and left.

Suspicions of why she might have done such a thing were already knotting his stomach. But he wasn't yet ready to acknowledge them. Instead, he picked up the phone and called the front desk. The sleepy clerk confirmed what Jim already knew. Terri had checked out hours earlier.

After replacing the receiver on the cradle, Jim took one last look around the suite. Then, with slow steps, he started back down the hall. Perhaps she'd left some sort of message for him in his room and he'd missed it. If so, it would probably be an angry note, but that would be better than nothing.

Once back in his own quarters, he began a methodical search. He didn't find anything until he picked the robe out of the bathtub. There, near the drain, he found his crumpled, water-stained business card.

He stared at it. He didn't need a note of explanation from Terri. This told the whole story.

Feeling faintly sick, he sat down heavily on the edge of the tub and stared at the card. What a fool he'd been! Terri Genetti was the first woman he'd cared about in what seemed a lifetime, and now he might well have lost her. And it was his own damn fault, because he'd been too much of a coward to level with her.

Seven

I hate to say it, but you look worse than you did last week after your going-out-of-business sale. Didn't you have fun at Hearthwood?"

"No," Terri replied. "No fun at all." The lifeless tone in which she spoke the words made Bonnie lift an eyebrow.

"You didn't meet anybody interesting?"

"Oh, the place was full of interesting people. I was the dull one," Terri said, combing a shaky hand through her dark hair.

"What do you mean?"

"Let's drop the subject."

Bonnie turned back to the box of sweaters she was unpacking. It was a slow Monday morning, and there were no customers in Rainbow Rags. For a few moments she worked in silence while Terri leaned back against the counter by the cash register and sipped out of the Styrofoam cup she held.

Finally Terri cleared her throat. "There is one thing I'll say about my weekend at Hearthwood. It made me realize I have to look to the future—not the past." And it couldn't have been truer. On the drive home, she'd realized that the only way she could bring her roiling emotions under control was to give herself something new to think about.

Bonnie glanced up and grinned. "That's the spirit. I'm glad you're finally admitting you have a future."

Terri nodded. "I'm not going to let this thing knock me flat. I've been thinking about a plan, and I'd like your opinion."

Bonnie held up a blue and red cotton knit sweater and cocked her head to look at it from an angle. "Fire away— I'm all ears."

"I want to pick up my business again. But, of course, I'll have to start on a very limited basis. What do you think of those carts that malls rent to small entrepreneurs?"

Bonnie pursed her lips. "They're cute. And since the holiday season is coming up, this would be a good time of year to try one."

"Exactly what I was thinking, and because they're oriented toward craftsmen, I thought I'd talk to one of my suppliers. He puts up attractively packaged homemade preserves and relishes, and I could do some breads and sweet rolls myself. That would cut down on overhead."

"But it would mean you'd be at the cart all day and in the kitchen all night," Bonnie pointed out.

"Yes, but I'm willing to do just about anything to get back on my feet."

Bonnie studied her friend. "It sounds like a good idea— but an awful lot of work. I know how independent you are, but would you be insulted if I offered to stake you—say, a thousand dollars?"

"Oh, I couldn't accept...."

"Come on. We're friends, aren't we? And I'd really like to help."

As Terri stared at the warmhearted young woman, tears came to her eyes. "Oh, Bonnie, I'm so lucky to have you.

But I wasn't telling you all this so you'd offer to lend me money."

"I know that. Just remember that you've done things for me that have really made a difference in my profit margin."

"Like what?"

"Like the window displays you designed for me. They really brought in the customers. Actually, I probably owe you this money."

Terri tried to refuse again, but her friend wouldn't take no for an answer.

"Let's stop discussing money and get onto something else. Are you thinking about staying here in Sommerset Mall?"

A defiant look came into Terri's green eyes. "Not after the way they've treated me. No, I think I'll talk to the management at Montgomery Mall."

"But they're going to ask for references. Do you think Sommerset will give you a good recommendation?"

Terri wrinkled her brow. That was the part of the equation she hadn't yet figured out. Before she could frame an answer, a deep male voice said behind her, "I'm certain the management will write Ms. Genetti an excellent letter—if that's what she really wants."

Both women turned their heads in surprise. Standing just inside the threshold of the shop, wearing a dark overcoat that emphasized his tall, virile good looks, was Jim Holbrook.

While Bonnie eyed him with undisguised appreciation, Terri scowled—as much at her own feminine reaction to the man as at his presence. Despite her anger, she felt the tug of overwhelming attraction that had drawn her to him in the first place. From the way he was looking at her now, she suspected that he hadn't forgotten a single searing moment of what had happened between them. Blurting out the words in overreaction to what she considered her own weakness, she inquired in a gritty voice, "And just how long have you been standing there eavesdropping?"

Aghast, Bonnie looked from one to the other. "Terri," she protested. "This is James Holbrook, the president of T. & H. Associates."

"How do you happen to know that?" Terri asked, wishing she had possessed that piece of information before last weekend.

Jim answered the question. "When Ms. Foster originally applied for retail space here, I happened to sit in on her interview. I've kept tabs on her progress, and I must say I'm very impressed," he added, glancing around the attractively turned out shop.

The mildly delivered explanation served only to shorten Terri's fuse, since it seemed to imply an unflattering comparison between her own failed business and her friend's successful one.

Jim caught the expression on her face. "I'm not here to see Ms. Foster, Terri. I'm here because I need to talk to you."

Again Bonnie looked from one strained face to the other. "Do the two of you know each other?" she asked in puzzlement.

"We met this weekend," Jim said wryly.

A light bulb seemed to go off behind Bonnie's blue eyes. "I see. Well, if you'll excuse me, I have some work to do." With that she picked up the box of sweaters and scurried into the stockroom.

In the ensuing silence, Terri and Jim stared at each other. "I have nothing to say to you—now or ever," she said finally in a biting tone.

"Don't I get any points for spending the morning tracking you down?" Jim countered, taking a step toward her. "Believe me, it wasn't easy. When you weren't at home, I didn't know where to look, until I remembered your mentioning your friend Bonnie."

Terri would have shrunk back if she hadn't already been leaning against the glass display case by the cash register. Since it was impossible to do anything else, she faced him defiantly. "If you're so good at detective work, then you must have figured out why I don't want to have anything more to do with you. You lied to me."

"I never told you anything that was untrue."

"No. You just neglected to mention a few pertinent details."

Jim slipped a finger inside his collar and glanced uncomfortably at the curtain beyond which Bonnie had disappeared. "Could we discuss this someplace else?" He checked his watch. "It's almost lunchtime. Why don't we go get a bite? I'm sure we could find somewhere private up Old Georgetown Road."

"There's nothing you have to say to me that I'd want to hear. And I have no intention of sitting down to a meal—or anything else—with you," Terri shot back.

Jim took a deep breath and continued in a low, urgent voice. "Surely after this weekend, you owe me the chance to explain."

For just a moment as she stared into his eyes, which burned with emotion, Terri felt something inside her chest contract. He really did look upset. Then she deliberately hardened her heart. He'd fooled her once, but he wasn't going to do it again. "I certainly don't want to think about the weekend," she retorted in a hoarse whisper. "You knew who I was the whole time. Did it amuse you to take advantage of me?"

Jim blanched. "For the record, I didn't know who you were at first. Remember, you wouldn't tell me anything but your first name."

That was true, Terri conceded silently. But what difference did it really make?

"And if you think back," he continued, "you'll realize I tried to tell you who I was at the buffet breakfast—but you were so worked up about T. & H. that I knew I couldn't identify myself without losing you."

"I don't want to hear any more of your explanations. In fact, if you keep harassing me, I'm going to call the police."

Jim struggled to control his temper. He put his hands in his pockets so that she wouldn't see the white knuckles of his clenched fists. Before he spoke again, he took a deep breath. "Obviously, this is not the time or the place to have a rational discussion with you."

"So we finally agree on something."

It was all he could do to keep from striding across the shop and shaking her. Instead, he seared her with a long, fiery look, then turned on his heel and stalked out.

As she watched him march past the mall's center court, Terri tried to stop herself trembling. She didn't know whether she was shaking with relief that he'd finally gone or with some other emotion. As she tried to get a hold on herself, Bonnie poked her bright curls out from behind the curtains. "Well, from what I could hear, that was quite a little scene," she murmured.

"I'm sorry you got dragged into that," Terri apologized. "Are you all right?"

"As a matter of fact—no. I think I'd better go home."

"And leave me wondering just exactly what happened this weekend at Hearthwood?"

"I'm afraid in this case you'll just have to use your imagination." As she spoke, Terri snatched her coat and purse off the chair. "I'll call you later, when I'm more coherent."

Terri had planned to stop at the Montgomery Mall management office and discuss their rental plan for carts. Instead, she went straight home and spent the next hour pacing back and forth in the living room, trying to work off the nervous energy generated by her encounter with Jim. When she'd left Hearthwood, she'd never wanted to see the

man again. Until this morning at Bonnie's, she'd told herself she'd be able to cope with the situation. But seeing Jim
away from the fantasy setting had changed things somehow. It had brought him into the framework of her every-
day reality. And it wasn't so easy to banish the image of his
tall, striking figure from her mind.

When she opened the phone directory to look up the
number of Montgomery Mall, she knew that it was no use
calling today. In her present state, her voice was not going
to project the image of a confident businesswoman.

But if she stayed at home, brooding, she would go to
pieces, and she wasn't going to allow herself to do that.
Resolutely she got out her cookbooks and took them into
the living room. It was a comfortable room, with a coun-
try-style love seat and sofa that she'd covered herself in a
small burgundy print. The coffee table on which she set the
books was an old cobbler's bench. She'd reupholstered in a
matching floral chintz the Victorian occasional chairs,
castoffs from her grandmother's attic.

After settling into the love seat, she began to look for favorite recipes that could be adapted to mass production if
she got the go-ahead on her business plans. But first she'd
have to retest them on a small scale to determine whether
each was as good as she remembered. In fact, it might not
be such a bad idea to give the Montgomery Mall management a sample of the wares she intended to sell.

The thought gave her a new feeling of purpose. After se-
lecting the things she was going to try that afternoon, she
made a grocery list and made a quick trip to the store, where
she bought flour, sugar, nuts and fruit. When she returned,
she changed into jeans and a flannel shirt and began to mix
up a batch of cranberry bread. After getting the loaf into the
oven, she started on homemade gingersnaps.

Glad of the chance to focus on something other than her
anger, Terri worked steadily until after dark.

As she opened the oven and removed the last batch of cookies, she inhaled deeply. The warm, spicy fragrance made her apartment smell as inviting as a bakery. With a feeling of accomplishment, she stood back and surveyed her handiwork.

She hadn't eaten since dinner the night before. Suddenly she realized that she was hungry, and reached for a gingersnap she'd rejected as a little too brown around the edges. When the doorbell rang she was too caught up in her own activities to wonder who it might be. Wiping her hands on her apron, she started for the living room. When she opened the front door, she was abruptly rocketed back to the distressing emotions of the morning.

"Don't slam the door on me," Jim pleaded as he took a step forward and put a foot over the threshold. "I have to talk to you."

Instinctively she tried to do exactly what he'd asked her not to. But the gesture was useless. His foot prevented it. Although she saw him wince, he held his ground and pushed the door back open. A moment later he'd stepped inside and closed it behind him.

"Does your place always smell this good?" he inquired, taking a deep, appreciative breath.

"Go away and leave me alone."

He shook his head. "I left this morning because I didn't want to create a scene in front of your friend. But we've got to talk, Terri. So you might as well make your mind up to it." He had already unbuttoned his coat and draped it across the back of one of the Victorian chairs. He looked around with interest at the apartment.

"This is really quite charming," he murmured.

"Well, don't bother making yourself comfortable."

Ignoring her sharp words, he sat down on the sofa. Terri stood staring at him. He must have come straight from the office. He was still wearing the business suit, white shirt and dark tie he'd had on that morning.

She shouldn't care what Jim Holbrook thought. Nevertheless, Terri was suddenly unhappily conscious of her own appearance. She'd been working like a galley slave all afternoon, and it showed, she thought as she glanced down at her well-worn jeans and stained apron. It had been a gift from Bonnie, and the legend across the front read, I Aim to Please.

Jim eyed the words but didn't comment. She could just imagine what was going through his mind.

He got up and sauntered into the kitchen. "You certainly have been busy. Do you always bake after you've squashed a lover's ego?" Reaching out, he picked up a sugar cookie she'd spent ten minutes decorating with red and green icing and took a bite. "This is delicious. I haven't eaten anything all day."

"That's nothing to me. And for your information," Terri snapped, "that cookie was intended for the manager at Montgomery Mall."

Jim's eyebrows shot up. "Is he a friend of yours?"

Terri snatched the half-eaten sweet out of his hand. "Don't be ridiculous! I'm going to see him about renting one of those carts."

"A cart? Why would you want one of those?"

"So I can get back into business. Why do you think?"

Jim shifted his weight as he studied the defiant glitter in her green eyes. "You intend to sit next to a cart all day and bake cookies all night? That's crazy. You'd burn yourself out within a month."

That was exactly what Bonnie had said—which only made Terri more determined. "Don't underestimate me. I've worked night and day before. I can do it again."

"I don't doubt that. But there's no reason you should," he said gently. He reached out and touched her shoulder, but she flinched and turned away.

"I'd appreciate it if you'd leave my apartment," she said, gritting her teeth.

"I will, just as soon as I've told you what I came for."

Terri sighed. "Then make it quick."

"Could we go back into the living room and sit down for a civilized conversation? I didn't get much sleep last night, and I've had a hard day."

So he hadn't slept much. Did that mean he'd awakened shortly after she'd left? she wondered. The speculation reminded her of what had passed between them less than twenty-four hours ago. Looking up, she caught the intensity of his gaze and realized he must be thinking the same thing.

Trying to maintain an air of unconcern, Terri shrugged to show her acquiescence. She supposed that the sooner she let him speak his piece, the sooner he'd go away and leave her alone to lick her wounds in private.

When he'd once again settled his long body on the sofa, he looked across the room, noting dryly that Terri had perched uneasily on the most distant chair. "Montgomery Mall is one of our rivals. Did you pick it because of that?"

"I picked it because it's near my home—and because I didn't want to have anything more to do with T. & H. Associates. That should be obvious."

He sighed. "I was hoping you'd give us—actually, I mean me—another chance."

"Why in the world should I?"

"Because I can offer you what you want."

"That sounds interesting." Her voice dripped with sarcasm. "And what is it that you think I want?"

"An opportunity to get your store back," he answered without blinking.

"T. & H. already made it clear that I can't do that."

"I've done some checking. Actually, the space hasn't yet been rented to anyone else."

"You must know that I can't afford to start again on that scale." Uncomfortably, Terri crossed her ankles and looked down at them. Just thinking about her old store standing gutted and empty made her feel sick.

Jim leaned forward. "You could open up again there if you had a loan."

"I tried every bank in the area. My credit just isn't good enough without the Gourmet Unlimited umbrella."

"It would be good enough for a certain type of loan—if I underwrote you."

Terri blinked. Had she heard him right? "Now, let me get this straight. *You* are personally willing to do what your company repeatedly told me was impossible? Now, why would that be? It couldn't be a good business decision."

"Not necessarily. I checked the records. Your store was doing very well before Gourmet Unlimited pulled the rug out from under you."

Terri laughed mirthlessly. "So why couldn't your company come to that conclusion?"

He raked a hand through his hair. "Because many of the decisions that have to be made on a corporate level look different on an individual basis."

Terri's face reddened. Stiff with indignation, she said, "Oh, I see. You mean when the corporate president is involved with the owner of the store that's flopped, his point of view changes."

Jim's own neck grew red. "That's not how I'd put it."

"Then don't keep me in the dark. How *would* you put it?"

Clearing his throat, he steepled his fingers. "Although it's not widely known, some years ago I established a fund to encourage small businesses that might not be able to qualify for loans through normal channels. The program is very selective, and in the past five years we've made grants to only ten companies. However, I spent the afternoon studying your records, and it looks as though you would easily qualify to be the eleventh."

Terri digested this new information for several minutes. The thought of getting her shop back was certainly tempting. But she knew that this wasn't the simple business proposition that Jim was making it sound like. Uncertainly, she twisted her fingers in the fringe of the pillow beside her. Glancing up, she saw Jim's eyes following the nervous movement. "And your personal feelings have nothing to do with this?"

"I'm not going to lie to you."

"That's refreshing."

He gripped the edge of the couch. The woman sitting across from him radiating hostility was very volatile, and he'd promised himself that he was going to keep his temper, no matter what she threw in his direction. Right now it wasn't easy. Only the knowledge of how much he'd hurt her allowed him to continue in something approaching a calm voice. "I told you up at Hearthwood that it's been a long time since I let myself care about a woman. I won't tell you my feelings aren't confused right now. But one thing I do know—I don't want things between us to end before they really get started."

Terri folded her arms across her chest. "Any personal relationship between us *has* ended. And since I know your offer isn't motivated strictly by business concerns, I can't accept it."

Jim sat there for a moment, hoping his emotions didn't show on his face. Then he stood up. "The offer of a loan is strictly business. But I can see that you're not in any shape to make a decision right now. So I'll leave."

Terri didn't reply.

"But I do have to tell you that there's another tenant interested in the space," Jim continued. "So I'd need to hear from you by the middle of the week."

Was he trying to pressure her? Terri wondered. If so, the tactic was working. The thought of someone else setting up shop in what had been her store was disturbing.

"Let me know if you change your mind." With that Jim walked to the door, opened it and stepped out into the hall.

It was almost twenty minutes after he left before Terri felt able to get off the chair where she'd sat, defying him. Her legs felt rubbery—from the shock of his offer and of having him in her apartment—and she suspected they wouldn't support her weight. But at last she managed to get to her feet. She was suddenly glad the kitchen was full of dirty bowls and pans, because that gave her something to do. As if it were her mission in life to clean cookie sheets, she began to scrub off burn marks that hadn't bothered her before. But none of this feverish activity could keep her mind off what had just happened in her living room.

What were the real motives behind his offer? she asked herself. Did he care more about her than she'd imagined? The idea was so heart-wrenchingly tempting that she couldn't even let herself consider it. He had hurt her, and she wasn't going to let it happen again. If he thought he could buy her, he had another think coming. No one could do that. Still, Terri found herself imagining what it would be like to have a chance at making another go of her shop. What would she call it if it were a truly independent enterprise? she mused as she squeezed dishwashing liquid into a mixing bowl and turned on the hot water.

The speculation brought her up short. How could her business be an independent enterprise if Jim Holbrook were making the loan? And why was she even allowing herself to think in these terms?

By the next morning Terri had tossed her way through her second sleepless night. In fact, the tangled sheets and scattered pillows made it look as if it had survived a hurricane, she thought as she glanced ruefully back at her bed. If she went on this way much longer, she'd make herself sick. And then she'd really be in no shape to start another business. Although pride had kept her from discussing Jim with

Bonnie yesterday, now she realized that she had to talk to someone about the situation.

"Would it be imposing on you if I came in and bent your ear?" she asked Bonnie over the phone after she'd fixed herself a cup of coffee.

"Not at all. You must know that I'm dying of curiosity."

"Well, hold on. I'll be in around ten to satisfy some of that."

When Terri arrived at Rainbow Rags, Bonnie turned over the cash register to her part-time assistant. "I could use a soda," she told her friend. "Why don't we go out and get drinks at one of the food stands?"

Terri agreed. Now that she was actually standing in front of Bonnie, the thought of telling her enough of what had happened so that she could ask her advice was a bit daunting, and she didn't mind postponing the moment of truth for a little while longer.

As they brought their sodas over to one of the round white tables arranged among the ficus trees in the mall's center court, Bonnie shot Terri a knowing smile.

"You look as though you've changed your mind about leveling with me. You don't have to tell me a thing, you know. Just keep in mind that with my imagination running unchecked, I've probably come up with something much juicier than the truth."

"Then maybe I'd better come clean with you," Terri muttered under her breath. But instead of starting to speak, she took a sip of her Coke and stared glumly at the grate from which a ficus tree grew, as though the answer to her problem might be found among the chewing gum wrappers and cigarette butts.

Bonnie looked sympathetically at Terri's slumped shoulders. "Do you want to hear what I've already figured out?" After waiting several moments for a reply, she continued. "Obviously, you and Jim Holbrook did more than play tennis at Hearthwood."

"That's right," Terri admitted. "He never bothered to tell me who he really was. But that didn't stop him from coming on like Don Juan."

"He's a very attractive guy. I wouldn't mind being the object of his desire. But somehow I never thought that he was quite that type. If anything, he seems rather conservative."

Terri eyed her friend. Bonnie's flamboyant looks had often invited male attention. "You mean, he never flirted with you?" she asked somewhat incredulously.

"Never a flicker. And not because I didn't try to stir up some interest."

"Oh." Terri mulled over that piece of information. Actually, it did fit in with what Jim had told her about himself.

"You know, there are a lot of guys who would take advantage of a power situation with a woman who happens to be a business associate. He made it clear that he didn't mix business with pleasure." Bonnie paused and gave her friend a direct look. "Are you sure he knew who you were when the two of you met?"

Terri opened her mouth to speak, then hesitated. As Jim had pointed out, she'd practically made a game out of not telling him her name. Of course, by the following day, he'd known, but they'd already come close to making love in front of her television set.

"Well?" Bonnie persisted.

"Probably not."

Bonnie waited until a young woman pushing a stroller had passed by their table. When the shopper was out of earshot, she asked, "What did he say about it?"

"That he was afraid of losing me," Terri answered in a low, strained voice.

"That sounds promising."

Terri shook her head. "Don't make too much of it. I just can't see myself getting involved with him romantically again."

Her friend didn't comment. But the look in her eye told Terri that she had her doubts.

"If he'd just go away and leave me alone, I could cope with the situation," Terri continued. "But last night he came over and made me a very tempting business proposition."

Bonnie opened the top of her paper cup and reached inside for a piece of ice. "What was it?" she asked as she popped a small cube into her mouth.

"He wants to make me a loan." She summarized the offer Jim had laid before her.

When Terri finished, Bonnie's eyebrows were raised high. "But that's just the kind of thing you've been hoping for!"

Terri sighed. "I know. And if it had come from anyone else but Jim Holbrook, I'd grab it. But—"

"But what? What difference does it make where it comes from?"

"Don't you see? How can I feel that this is a legitimate business arrangement when I spent the weekend with him?"

"He knows you're not that type. Let's look at this thing objectively."

Terri shook her head. "All right," she agreed.

"Let's start with his business reputation. He hasn't gotten where he is by being a softhearted fool. If he says he thinks your business deserves a chance, then he's not lying."

Terri nodded. The argument made sense. Before she'd decided to locate in Sommerset Mall, she'd inquired at the bank about T. & H. and had been assured that they were known in the business community for their acumen.

"And what about you? You told me that you could have made a go of your store if Gourmet Unlimited hadn't left you holding an empty grocery bag—or if that gorgeous brother of yours had been able to come through with a loan.''

"I still think I could make a success of it," Terri admitted, "if I were given half a chance.''

"Well, Jim Holbrook *is* giving you that chance, and I think you'd be a fool not to take it. Letting the guy underwrite a loan for you doesn't mean you have to sleep with him. In fact, your previous relationship doesn't have to enter into this arrangement at all. It's strictly business.''

Terri was silent while she considered Bonnie's words. What her friend was saying made sense. Had she allowed her emotions to cloud her thinking last night? Perhaps she should reconsider Jim's offer. But that meant she was going to have to swallow her pride and call him—quickly.

Eight

Making that call was one of the hardest things Terri had ever had to do. She picked up the receiver and put it down four times before she could force herself to go ahead and dial the number. Even then her fingers trembled as they punched out the correct numbers.

"Mr. Holbrook's office," a female voice answered.

Jim had used the word "motherly" to describe his secretary. On the phone, however, she sounded crisp and efficient.

"May I speak to Mr. Holbrook, please?"

"Who shall I say is calling?"

"Ms. Genetti."

"Oh, yes." Terri detected a definite change for the warmer in the woman's impersonal voice. "I'll put you through right away."

A moment later Terri heard Jim's deep, authoritative tones. "Terri! I'm glad you called."

She cleared her throat. "Yes, well. I was thinking about your business proposition last night, and I wonder if we could discuss it further."

"Of course. Would you like to meet for dinner?"

"No."

There was a long pause. "What if I come to your office?" Terri finally suggested.

"Just a moment while I check my schedule. I'm swamped until six-thirty. But I could see you then, if that's not too late."

"That would be fine," Terri replied primly.

"Do you know where T. & H. is located?"

She gave the northern Virginia address that she'd looked up in the phone book.

"Well, I'll see you at six-thirty, then," Jim said as he signed off.

When Terri put down the phone, her hands were shaking and her mouth was dry. I'd better get a hold on myself between now and the time I see the man, she thought. When she met with Jim, she didn't want to feel any more at a disadvantage than she already was. Because of that—and to give herself something to focus on—Terri selected her clothing carefully. This was a business meeting, not a romantic rendezvous, and she wanted Jim to know it.

After a lot of thought, she selected a gray pin-striped suit that made her feel practically armor-plated. To soften it a bit, she matched the jacket with a dusty-rose blouse that tied at the neck in a floppy bow. She completed the outfit with black patent leather pumps and a matching purse. As she inspected her reflection in the mirror, she considered taking a briefcase to complete the picture of no-nonsense professionalism that she wanted to project. But she discarded the idea, since there really wasn't anything to put in the briefcase. She knew Jim had his own copy of her records and had already gone over them.

Terri glanced at the clock. It was four and possibly too early to leave. But rush-hour traffic between the Maryland suburbs and northern Virginia was unpredictable. Better to sit on the beltway for thirty minutes than to be late.

As it turned out, she arrived early. Not wanting to appear overanxious, she sat in her car, trying to read a magazine she'd brought along. But there was no way she could make her mind focus on the lines of print. Finally she gave up and watched the office workers leaving the building. As the parking lot emptied, she began to feel faintly nervous about meeting with Jim so late. The thought hadn't occurred to her before, but the building was bound to be almost deserted. That was just silly, she told herself as she unlocked her car door and climbed out. Jim Holbrook certainly wasn't going to make passes in his office—or at least she didn't think he would.

Inside the building the lights had been turned down, so the corridors were dim and shadowy. As Terri stepped out of the elevator, she realized that T. & H. Associates occupied the whole fourth floor. But there was no one at the desk in the carpeted reception area. Would she have to wander around looking for Jim's office? she asked herself.

Her brow was just furrowing at the thought when she saw him striding toward her from the end of the hall on her left.

"How did you know I was here?" she exclaimed.

"There's a photoelectric cell that we turn on after hours—just as a precaution when someone wants to work late. Your arrival was announced by a buzzer."

"How high-tech," Terri commented.

"Not really. It's fairly commonplace these days."

They stood appraising each other for a moment. From the wry expression in his eyes as he took in her buttoned-up suit, she suspected he knew exactly why she'd chosen it.

He, on the other hand, looked more informal than the last time she'd seen him. He'd removed his jacket, and his shirt sleeves were rolled up over his muscular, hair-roughened forearms. The sudden memory of how it had felt to be held in those arms and intimately caressed by those long-fingered hands made her swallow nervously.

She tried not to think about that, but she couldn't help reacting to the other physical details of his appearance. His collar was open at the throat and he'd loosened his tie, so she could see his strong, tanned neck and the hollow where it met his chest. Only two days earlier she'd kissed that spot passionately. She could vividly remember the salty taste of his skin and the way he'd drawn in his breath with pleasure at the stroking of her tongue against his flesh.

"How about coming down to my office, where we can be more comfortable?" he invited her.

Wrapped up in heated memories, she was startled by his voice. In the context that her brain had been conjuring up, the suggestion could have been an invitation to dalliance.

"What?"

"We can sit down in my office and talk."

Terri struggled for a sense of proportion. She had made it clear that their physical relationship was over. So it must simply be her imagination that his voice sounded husky. "All right."

He seemed about to take her arm when he thought better of it and gestured back down the hallway before dropping his hand to his side. Silently she followed him to a mahogany door with a brass nameplate. Once inside, she looked around at the richly paneled walls, thick floor coverings and plush upholstery. Since she'd uncovered his identity, she'd realized that he was a very successful man—whatever else he might be. Now she was struck by the outward trappings of that success.

Despite her preparations for this meeting, as she heard Jim close the door behind them, she felt more than ever at a disadvantage.

"Sit down." He indicated an armchair close to his desk. "I don't know about you, but it's been a hard day, and I'd like a drink. Can I offer you something?"

He crossed over to a wall unit that matched the paneling. Terri had expected to see a bar with a bank of expensive liquor bottles. Instead, there was a small refrigerator. Terri could see that the interior was stocked with a variety of fruit juices. They looked tempting, but she didn't want to accept anything from Jim that might smack of hospitality.

"No thanks," she declined.

Shrugging, he pulled out a carton of grapefruit juice, poured the contents into a glass and added ice.

While Terri watched him take a hearty swallow, she gripped her purse. Why didn't he get to the point? Had he changed his mind? Or was he stalling?

He hadn't yet taken his seat. As he stood drinking his juice, she watched his Adam's apple bob, and then her gaze drifted down the length of his lean, muscular torso. Would she ever be able to look at him dispassionately? she wondered. Or would she always feel enveloped by the attraction he held for her? The emotions she couldn't turn off gave him power over her, and she resented the fact.

Then suddenly it dawned on her just how much power he really had. Almost from the moment they'd met, she'd been under his spell. He'd overwhelmed her with his lovemaking in a way she'd never dreamed was possible in real life. Now he was in a position to make or break her business. She didn't even have the protection of being an unknown quantity. In the intimacy of their relationship, she had told him things about herself that she would never have confided to a would-be business associate.

But none of that mattered, she assured herself, unconsciously sitting up straighter. If he had lured her here to change the conditions of his offer—to try to persuade her to resume their relationship—she would simply get up and walk out.

Taking his half-empty glass to his desk, Jim sat down in a comfortable-looking swivel chair and leaned back. "So, why did you reconsider, if I may ask?"

"It was my friend Bonnie Foster," Terri admitted frankly. "When I told her about your offer, she convinced me that I was being foolish."

Jim frowned. "And did you tell her about our... encounter?"

"Only in the most general terms," Terri replied stiffly. She certainly wasn't likely to confide the details of her weekend with Jim to anyone, not even her closest friend.

"Well, that's a relief. Despite what you think, Terri, what happened between us at Hearthwood had nothing to do with business. It was strictly between us, and no one else."

"You'd be embarrassed if anyone knew about it?"

"No. But I don't relish putting my personal life on public display."

She stared at him. The frank look he gave her made her realize that he'd just deliberately handed her a playing card. If he had power over her, she now had something to use against him if she wanted to. "Well, I'm not interested in going public either," she told him. "Perhaps we ought to get on with the details of the proposal."

Jim opened his desk and pulled out a large manila folder. "It's all in here. Why don't you have a look at it?"

"Thank you." Terri accepted the collection of papers and began to study the carefully spelled out terms of the agreement Jim was proposing.

He waited to see if she had any initial questions. When she didn't, he got out of his chair and walked over to the window, which overlooked a private park between the office buildings. It was dark now and globe lamps illuminated the meandering pathways. Dry leaves littered the ground under the trees and between the flower beds. Before he realized it, fall would be over and they'd be into the gray weather of winter. He hadn't paid much attention to the seasons in a long time, but now the thought of overcast skies and leafless trees depressed him.

He turned and glanced back at Terri. She was bent over the papers, completely absorbed in the words and numbers he'd spent a good part of yesterday putting together. Her preoccupation gave him a chance to study her. Her hair was pulled back into a French twist. Hungrily he gazed at her sleek, dark head and for a moment tenderly looked at the graceful curve of her neck. He remembered kissing the spot just under her ear and feeling the frantic beat of her pulse, which told him how much she wanted him. Would she ever come willingly into his arms again? If he thought she wasn't going to, he'd feel like throwing himself out this window.

But what he felt for her was stronger even than physical desire. He wanted to help and protect her. She had taken an important step back toward him. Maybe now that it seemed as if she might let him assist her, there was hope that she'd also allow him back into her life.

On that thought, he crossed to his desk and looked at the stack of correspondence waiting to be answered. He could use this time to catch up on some of it. But he was much too restless to do anything useful.

At that moment Terri looked up from her reading. "So far this looks very fair," she admitted almost grudgingly. "But it's hard to really study it under these conditions."

"You could take it home with you. But I'd need your decision by the day after tomorrow. The tenant I spoke of is pressing hard for that space, and it wouldn't be fair to put him off any longer than that."

"I understand." Terri gazed up at him as if trying to see beyond his words to what motivated them.

He carefully kept his expression neutral. He didn't want her to know how badly he'd like to see her sign those papers—and give him a second chance.

Terri did take the papers home with her. It was a relief to

escape from Jim's office. While she'd been sitting near his desk, trying to look cool and professional, the words on the document he'd given her had been nothing but a blur before her eyes. She'd thought she'd be able to concentrate better in the privacy of her apartment. But no such luck. Every time she picked up the contract to study it, she managed to get no further than the second or third page before her usually sharp mind started to wander.

Yet from what she could tell, everything looked very acceptable. What's more, whatever was in the contract, she certainly wasn't going to be worse off than she was now. And now that reopening was within her grasp, she was eager to get started. Before she could give herself any more time to worry about what the contract might imply, she signed it and mailed it to Jim's office.

He must have been waiting for it, because two days later she received a call from Mr. Patterson, the manager of Sommerset Mall, welcoming her back into the fold and telling her that while she waited for the loan to be processed, the mall would advance her five thousand dollars to restock.

She hadn't expected such quick action. Feeling a little overwhelmed, she sent Jim a note of thanks.

The next few days were a round of perpetual activity. Some of her stock would have to be delivered by mail. But much of it was available through local distributors and craftsmen. These Terri called, and in some cases went to visit personally.

While the shop stood empty, the mall management had covered its windows with decorative paper. To this Terri affixed a sign announcing her reopening a week from Monday. She wanted to be back in business as soon as possible before her old customers got out of the habit of stopping by. But if she was going to make her self-imposed deadline, she would have to work like a beaver.

In truth, she welcomed the excuse to be so busy. Despite everything, thoughts of Jim kept popping into her head. She found that the best way to keep that from happening at night as she lay in bed was for her to have worked herself to the point of exhaustion during the day.

There were so many things she needed to do. Since she wanted everything about the shop to look fresh and new, she splurged on paint and wallpaper and spent the greater part of the week redecorating. And she even put together a sign with the new name of her shop. She decided on Gourmet Galore. Although she knew it was a bit hokey, she felt it did have a certain ring. And the sign she'd made featured Gs that were cornucopias overflowing with specialty foods.

The effect was quite charming, she mused as she admired the finished product. But stock still had to be attractively arranged on the shelves and in the window.

She would have to spend the weekend doing that and taking care of the millions of little tasks that needed attention.

Although Bonnie stopped by and tried to get her to take a lunch break on the Saturday before her opening, Terri declined.

"I've already packed myself a sandwich," she explained. "I think I'll just eat that while I try to figure out an eye-catching way to set up the herbal tea display."

"If you don't stop pushing yourself, you're going to be a burnout case by the time Monday rolls around," her friend warned.

Terri only laughed. "Don't worry. Right now I feel higher than a kite. It's so good to be back in business."

"Well, then, what about dinner?"

"I'll probably work late and eat when I get home."

"Are you trying to avoid me, by any chance?" Bonnie asked quizzically.

Terri wiped a smudge of dirt off the back of her hand. "Of course not. How could you think that? Monday eve-

ning we'll go to the Brass Rooster and I'll buy you a cele-
bratory drink."

"It's a deal," Bonnie agreed with a grin. "But don't work
yourself into a hospital bed."

For answer Terri merely flipped her dust rag at her friend,
who exited laughing.

An hour later Mr. Patterson poked his head in the door.
"Say, you're making great progress," he said approvingly.

Terri did her best to look friendly. Three weeks ago he'd
told her unequivocally that she was going to lose her store.
Now he was all smiles. It was amazing, she mused, how a
good word from the president of the company could change
things.

"I wouldn't have thought it was possible for you to open
again so quickly. But it looks as though you're going to
make your deadline," he said, glancing around at the new
decor. "You've really spruced things up, haven't you," he
added, inspecting the fresh paint and wallpaper. "It looks
great."

When he was gone, Terri looked around, trying to decide
what to do next. She'd been putting off shelving the canned
goods, because they were heavy. But maybe it was time to
tackle that.

After dragging several boxes from the stockroom, she
pried the tops open with a heavy screwdriver and began
lifting out decorative tins of olive oil. After they were in
place, she turned to the shipment that contained gourmet
soups.

She was just lifting out a can of vichyssoise when a knock
at the door made her turn her head.

Was it Mr. Patterson—or Bonnie? she wondered.

When Jim Holbrook poked his dark head through the
opening and smiled at her, she almost dropped the can of
soup.

"Sorry. I didn't mean to startle you. But I had some business in the management office and thought I'd stop by to see how you were doing."

As he spoke, he stepped inside and closed the door behind him. "I see you've been busy."

"I still am." It had been over a week since she'd seen Jim. Despite everything, her heart started to pound. They stood there staring at each other, and Terri pushed back a lock of hair, suddenly conscious of how she must look. She'd been working almost nonstop all day. Her jeans and T-shirt were streaked with the paint she'd put on the walls yesterday. And she hadn't bothered to do anything more with her hair than catch it at the back of her neck with a rubber band.

"Patterson tells me you're planning on opening Monday," Jim observed.

"Yes, if I can get these shelves arranged in time. But it isn't going to be easy."

"No. You must be tired by now." He took off his jacket and began rolling up his sleeves. "Here, let me give you a hand."

Terri jumped to her feet and put out her palm. "That isn't necessary, really."

"I know. But I'd like to." He looked at the large cartons at her feet. "How did you get those out here?"

"I dragged them."

"That can't be good for your back. If you hurt it, you're likely to end up in bed—not running a store. Tell me what else you need, and I'll bring it out for you."

Terri wanted to protest again, but she knew what he was saying was true. Things would be a lot easier if he carried the heavy cartons out for her. And anyway, she didn't think she could stop him. He was already heading for the stockroom.

Jim brought out the boxes that she needed, but he didn't stop there. When she unfolded the step stool so that she could get to the top shelves, he shook his head. "I can reach those. Just show me what you want up there and I'll take care of them.''

It was easier to let him have his way than to argue with him, Terri told herself. Maybe if it had been earlier in the day, she wouldn't have caved in. But she'd been working hard since eight that morning, and she was beginning to feel awfully tired.

For the next hour, they worked side by side. To Terri's surprise, the job went twice as fast as if she'd been struggling alone.

Jim stopped and brushed off his hands. There was a smudge across the formerly immaculate front of his white shirt, and before Terri could stop herself, she reached out to brush it off. When her fingers touched his chest, they froze as she realized what she was doing. Through the fabric she could feel the warmth of his body and the steady beat of his heart. His eyes locked with hers, and he reached up to capture her hand. ''You look beat,'' he murmured. ''And we've finished one whole side of the shop. How about taking a dinner break?''

''I don't have time for that.''

''As your business partner, I insist that you take care of your diet. Listen, why don't I go upstairs to the Gold Dragon and bring us back some carryout?''

Terri felt her mouth water. She hadn't stopped to eat since her hurried sandwich at lunch, and she *was* hungry. While she hesitated, torn between temptation and not wanting to accept Jim's hospitality, he began to name some dishes.

''I like Szechuan food myself. What about some Kung Pao chicken and some Mu Shi pork? And we could start with an order of hot and sour soup.''

The suggestions sounded wonderful, and Terri's acquiescence must have registered on her face.

''I'll be back in a few minutes,'' Jim told her, rolling down his sleeves as he turned toward the door.

For a moment, she almost called him back. She shouldn't be letting him do this for her. Then she shrugged. It was too late now, she admitted, so she might as well be civilized about it.

After disappearing into the tiny powder room to wash her hands and brush her hair, she pulled out the folding table that she sometimes used to exhibit place settings. She covered it with a bright flowered cloth, then got out decorator paper napkins and plates in a matching pattern. There were candles, she thought, glancing at the display to the right of the counter. But that would be going too far. Instead, she simply set up two folding chairs from the stockroom and sat down to wait.

When Jim came back, he cast an appreciative eye on the attractive little table. "I wasn't expecting anything quite this nice," he allowed as he brought over a brown paper bag and began taking out fragrant white cartons. There were six. As Terri gazed in surprise, he laughed. "Maybe my eyes were bigger than my stomach, but I couldn't resist the Szechuan green beans and the Kung Pao shrimp."

"Kung Pao shrimp. That's one of my brother Tony's favorites," Terri said, reaching over and forking out some of the gingery concoction.

Jim had sat down opposite her and began ladling out hot and sour soup into bowls he'd prudently brought from the restaurant. "You told me that you came from a family of six. How many brothers and sisters do you have?"

"Three brothers and two sisters."

While he watched her spoon up her soup, Jim waited for her to volunteer more information. When she didn't, he asked another question. "So where does Tony fit in the lineup?"

"I'm the youngest, and he's a year older."

"Is he in business, too?"

Terri had to laugh. "You might say that. He's into the business of haunting racetracks and gambling casinos."

He looked at her quizzically. "Oh, so I have the same tastes in food as the black sheep of your family?"

"Mmm-hmm."

The last news she'd had from Tony was his postcard from Florida. But she wasn't worried. Tony always landed on his feet, and he had a way of coming back into her life when she least expected it.

As Terri put down her soup spoon, she grimaced faintly, remembering that she hadn't been too proud to ask Tony for a loan when her business was going under. If he hadn't just taken a bad loss on a business venture himself, he would have been able to help her.

"I have the feeling your family was a big influence on you."

"Not the way you think. The Genettis are traditionalists. Except for Tony, they believe that a woman's role in life is to cook, take care of her husband and have babies. But I wanted more."

"Why?"

Terri laughed harshly. "Because of my oldest sister. She did everything she was supposed to, and her husband left her with three kids and no way to support them. She had a wonderful choice—either to go on welfare or come home and live with my parents."

"That's rough."

"Yes, it was. She's remarried now, and she's okay. But she had some pretty tough years." Terri paused. "When I was a teenager, I swore that would never happen to me. But the pressure my parents and almost everyone else put on me to conform was enormous. The only way I could escape was to go out on my own."

"So that's why the store meant so much to you?"

"Yes. And I never told anyone in my family that I was going out of business—except for Tony. I knew the rest of them would just say I should have found myself a husband instead of thinking I could make it in the business world."

He looked at her thoughtfully. What she had told him explained a lot.

"I don't know what got into me. I shouldn't have told you all that."

"I'm glad you did. You know, I have a favorite brother, too," Jim volunteered.

"Did he turn out to be a business tycoon, like you?" Terri asked, glad to shift the topic of conversation away from herself.

"I'd hardly call myself a tycoon."

"Oh, then what would you call yourself?"

He thought for a moment. "A businessman, I guess."

"A very successful one."

"You may not believe it, but what success I've achieved has just sort of crept up on me. I was too busy trying to make a go of our malls and to make sure our investors didn't lose their shirts to think about what I was going to get out of it personally. And to be honest, I've never considered myself as successful the way my brother is."

Terri couldn't hold back her interest in what made Jim tick. "What do you mean?"

"Dan's an artist. I was always envious of his talent for making beautiful things." Jim paused and looked around the small shop. "He's like you."

"Oh, you can hardly compare me to an artist."

"I'm serious. You have a magic touch with color and design. But even if someone hadn't walked into your store, they'd know that. You even dress with a put-together look that most women can't come close to."

Embarrassed, Terri glanced down at her paint-stained jeans and top. Ruefully she shook her head as she forked up some Kung Pao chicken. Unfortunately, she didn't look at it closely before putting it into her mouth. In the next moment, her teeth crunched down on one of the strong red peppers that were the hallmark of the dish but were never eaten by Westerners. Instantly her eyes began to water, her face flushed and she started to cough.

Jim knew right away what had happened. "Don't swallow it," he said as he rose from the table and dashed to the sink to get her a cup of water.

She had gotten the pepper out of her mouth, but she was still gasping and blinking back tears when he returned.

"Here."

He handed her the water, and she took a grateful gulp. Despite the cool liquid, her mouth still felt as if it was on fire. In reaction to the pepper, tears had welled up in her eyes and were spilling down her cheeks.

"I did that once," Jim sympathized. "It takes a little while to recover."

Unable to speak, Terri nodded. It seemed to be taking her forever. The tears that had started running down her cheeks were now gushing from her eyes, and her throat felt constricted.

Mortified by her reaction, she grabbed one of the paper napkins on the table and held it to her face. She wanted to say something, but she knew if she tried to speak, she would make an even greater fool of herself.

Jim stood by, watching her with concern and wondering what to do. He could see that her reaction was way out of proportion. The pepper had started her tears, but something much more complicated must be going on inside her now.

She had made it clear that she didn't want anything personal between them. But whether she liked it or not, there *was* something personal—very personal indeed. Unable to stop himself from responding to her distress, he reached down, pressed his palm against her cheek and pulled her face against his muscled midsection. At first she tried to free herself. As one hand stroked her hair and the other gently kneaded her tense shoulders, she stopped resisting the contact. But still the tears flowed.

Jim looked around the shop. In one corner was a pine bench, which he supposed Terri must use for displays. Right now it held a stack of newspaper. With one smooth motion he reached down and picked her up. Cradling her in his arms, he crossed to the bench, pushed the newspaper to the floor and sat down with her in his lap.

"Don't!" she choked out her response, trying again to push herself away.

"It's all right," he said soothingly, his lips inches from her ear. "Just relax. You'll feel better in a minute." He continued to murmur soft, reassuring words as his hands gentled her back and shoulders. Slowly, she did relax. And at last she stopped crying. As her tears receded, she was too embarrassed to lift her head from his broad shoulder.

"I don't know what got into me," she whispered.

"I think I do. You've been under a lot of pressure. Stress will do that to you sometimes."

"I'll bet you never burst into tears over a red pepper."

"No. But I've known the feeling."

"When?"

She felt him grow very still.

"Actually, I felt that way when I woke up at Hearthwood expecting to find you next to me and you were gone."

That couldn't be true, Terri thought. Surely it hadn't meant so much to him! Nevertheless, she lifted her tear-wet eyes to his, and for a moment they stared into each other's souls.

Nine

Terri, you don't know how much I've longed to hold you in my arms again," Jim murmured as he lowered his face to hers. He could no more stop himself from kissing her now than stop his heart from beating.

And it was the same for Terri. She hadn't wanted to admit it to herself, but she had missed him desperately. The thought that she would never feel his arms around her again had been so painful that she had tried to wipe it out of her mind. Now she turned her face up to his like a morning glory seeking light.

He had wanted to kiss her tenderly, but the moment his lips came down on hers, the hunger that had been gnawing at him took over. Or perhaps it had been fear—fear that he would never hold her like this again.

As his mouth ravished hers, he pulled her to him with a kind of desperation, almost as though he were hoping that he could make her want him by the sheer force of his will.

There was no need for him to overpower her. Terri might have been alarmed by the passion vibrating through him, but when his lips touched hers, she suddenly realized that she was starving for him just as he was for her.

Fiercely, she dug her fingers into the firm muscles of his shoulders even as her mouth responded to his demand. It was like the urgency of their first kiss, when he had dragged her off the dance floor and out into the shadows of the terrace. Then she'd only been imagining the ecstasy of his lovemaking. Now she knew the rapture she could find in his embrace.

"Oh, Terri," he groaned as his lips left hers to chart a random course across her fevered flesh.

His hands trembled as he cupped her face and tipped it up toward his. Her eyes were still luminous from the tears she'd shed. But they were also bright with quickly kindled passion. Instinctively he realized that in her present vulnerable state he could make her yield to him, if that was what he wanted.

It *was* what he wanted. But what about afterward? He knew she would hate herself later—and probably him as well.

Regretfully he put his hands on her shoulders and shifted her slightly away from him, experiencing a chill when he could no longer feel her warmth against his chest. And as he saw the startled expression on her face, he knew that she, too, felt that way.

"Terri," he said gently. "It's just the same between us as it's been right from the first. I want you so badly that I'm going to hate myself tonight. But the stakes are too high for me to take advantage of that just now."

Terri stared up at him, her hands still clinging to his shoulders.

Tenderly, he reached out and traced the upper curve of her lip. "What I told you was true," he continued as he gazed down into her green eyes. "I didn't know who you

were when we met. But I won't lie and say I didn't set out to
seduce you at Hearthwood. I wanted you from the moment
I saw you walk into the lobby." He straightened slightly.
"But I think I've paid for that mistake. And if there's anything I've realized over the past few days, it's that things are
never going to be right between us unless you trust me."

Terri didn't know how to respond. But Jim didn't seem to
require an answer.

"So I'll leave now. But," he said with a wry little smile,
"I'll be back. You can count on it." As he spoke, he carefully levered her off his lap and seated her next to him on the
bench. He got to his feet, tucked his loosened shirt into his
waistband and reached for his jacket. "Are you working
tomorrow?" he asked.

She nodded, still at a loss for words.

"You look exhausted. I'd like to come back and give you
a hand."

Terri finally found her voice. "Are you sure that's how
you want to spend your Sunday?"

Suddenly he grinned. "Yes, but you don't have to worry
about a replay of what just happened. I'll be a friend and a
helper, and that's all." He paused. "What's a good time?"

"Any time," she answered. "I'm going to get here by nine
and stay as long as it takes."

Jim was as good as his word. The next morning he
showed up with bagels and cream cheese and large Styrofoam containers of fresh coffee. And he worked straight
through with Terri until late in the afternoon. At four
o'clock the two of them stood in the center of the shop, inspecting the counters and shelves with satisfaction.

"It really does look good," Terri said, wiping her hands
on her jeans.

"Yes. You do have a flair for this sort of thing. What you
did with the tea was really clever. I would never have
thought of decorating a tree with the different tea bags."

Terri grinned. "Well, Christmas is just around the corner."

Jim turned and glanced toward the back room. Unlike the public area of the shop, it was a jumble of boxes and crates—many open, but some still untouched. Surprisingly, Terri seemed to be able to function in the disorder. But he was sure it was going to create a problem down the road. "Have you set up an inventory system yet?" he asked.

"No. I haven't had the time."

"I could put one together for you," he offered. "That sort of thing is my strong suit. My father owned a string of stores. I started working in the stockrooms when I was fourteen."

Terri considered the offer. It was tempting; she sometimes did run short of items that were in demand, and she had wasted a good deal of time trying to find merchandise that was buried at the bottom of the heap. But despite their truce, she hadn't forgotten Jim's tendency to take command. While they'd been stocking the shelves, he'd cheerfully let her give him directions, yet she'd sensed that sometimes he'd had to restrain his desire to take over. Gourmet Galore was going to be her business, and hers alone. Better that she do all her own work—and do it her way. "Thanks," she said, "but I don't want to impose."

"I wouldn't regard it as an imposition."

"I'd still rather wait and try to handle everything myself. Right now I'm feeling very possessive about this store."

He shrugged. "I guess I can understand that. But remember, I'm always willing to help. And right now, I'd like to celebrate with you by buying dinner. How about it?"

Terri couldn't bring herself to refuse. They'd had such a good day together, and Jim really had been wonderful. What's more, it was gratifying to have someone with whom she could share this new beginning. As he'd worked tirelessly beside her, Jim had seemed as excited about the reopening of the shop as she had herself. "Okay," she agreed, "but I'm not exactly dressed for a restaurant."

He glanced down at his own corduroy slacks and gray ragg sweater. "Neither am I, but there's a place in the mall that should accommodate us. Besides, Sunday afternoon is a pretty casual time."

Agreeing, Terri looked around for her purse and jacket. A few minutes later they were heading toward the other end of the mall. But when they reached the family restaurant near the entrance, the lights were off, and it was obvious that the place was closed. Jim frowned and then checked his watch. "I'd forgotten that they shut down early on Sunday."

Terri laughed. "You don't keep track of the hours of all the stores in your malls, do you?"

"Well, I'd like to." He took her arm. "Let's try the deli next to the bookstore. As I recall, they serve wonderful corned beef sandwiches."

The sight of the darkened restaurant had made Terri realize how hungry she really was. Immediately agreeing to Jim's suggestion, she walked back with him toward the center court. But once they were inside The Cornbeef Express, the counter attendant, who obviously hadn't recognized Jim, gave them an impatient look.

"I'm afraid we're just about to close up. I can make you sandwiches, if you're willing to take them out."

Terri wondered if Jim would let the boy know that he was the shop's landlord and insist that he give them VIP treatment. Instead, he shrugged and turned to Terri. "I'm going to have to write the management of this mall a letter about their shortcomings."

She grinned up at him, enjoying the private joke. "Let's just take something out. We can eat in the center court."

Jim agreed and they ordered. A few minutes later when they emerged, Jim was carrying a bag with sandwiches and some potato salad. Terri had the soft drinks, plastic cutlery, napkins and straws.

As she glanced at the round white tables near the fountain, she wondered why no one was sitting at any of them. Then she saw the uniformed attendants methodically turning the chairs upside down and realized that the whole mall must be closing.

"I'm afraid we're out of luck," Jim said, voicing her own thought.

They could go back to her shop. But she'd already spent so much time there and the place was so neatly arranged that the idea held little appeal. Would she be a fool to ask him to her apartment? Before she could answer the silent question, she heard herself suggesting, "Why don't we take the food back to my place?"

Jim gave her a surprised look. "I'd like that—if it wouldn't be any trouble."

Suddenly Terri remembered the bed she hadn't bothered to make that morning. But he wasn't going to see her bed, and the rest of the apartment was presentable.

Fifteen minutes later, she inserted the key in the lock of her front door. Terri had issued the invitation on impulse. Now as Jim followed her into her living room, she wondered again if it was such a good idea. But clearly Jim didn't have any doubts. He was already cheerfully carrying the paper bag full of food to the dining-room table.

As he brought out the sandwiches, Terri stepped into the kitchen. "You know, most of those baked goods I made the other day are in the freezer. Would you like some of my chocolate chip cookies for dessert?"

"Sounds wonderful."

"Then I'll put some out on the counter."

They'd been too busy to talk much during the day. Now, as they sat down across from each other in the silence of her apartment, both concentrated on their food.

What exactly did you say to a former lover who had become your silent business partner? Terri wondered. As she munched her sandwich, she glanced up at him from under lowered lashes. No matter how many times she had tried to talk herself out of it, she still felt the little *zing* of awareness that washed over her every time they were alone together. But tonight it was mixed with something else that she couldn't quite identify until she realized she was reacting to the shadows under his eyes and the slight droop of his broad shoulders. He looked worn-out, she observed with a pang of guilt. And it was her fault. After working hard since Monday and putting in extra hours getting that contract ready for her, he'd spent his entire weekend laboring in her store.

"I'm not sending you back to your office on Monday very rested, am I?" she said.

Jim set down his sandwich and rolled his shoulders. Then he turned his head slowly from side to side. "I'm all right. But it never ceases to amaze me that no matter how good shape you try to keep yourself in, when you use different muscles, they let you know it."

Terri had been hungry when they'd started eating. Now she knew she'd served herself too much potato salad and pushed her plate away. "Is your neck bothering you?"

"It does feel a little stiff."

"I probably shouldn't have let you do all the top shelves."

"It was easier for me than for you." Jim finished off the last of his cold drink. Then he slid back his chair. "Maybe a cup of coffee would make me feel better. Do you have instant?"

"Yes," Terri said, looking up from what remained of her drink. "I'll get some for you."

"You need to relax. I know how to boil water." With that, Jim turned and walked into the kitchen.

From where Terri sat at the dining-room table, she could see him filling the kettle at the sink. "The coffee's in the cabinet above you," she told him.

He opened the small door and looked inside. When he reached to get the jar, he winced, and she realized he must be in more pain than he'd admitted to. Quickly she carried her plate into the kitchen. Jim had just taken the kettle off the burner and was pouring boiling water over coffee crystals in a mug.

"Listen," Terri told him as she arranged some cookies on a dish, "it looks to me as if you have a pulled muscle. My brother used to get those, and he taught me a way to make it feel better."

Jim turned slowly back to her. "You don't have to do anything like that. I can just go home and put a heating pad on it."

"Yes, but by that time it'll be too late." Without giving him time to protest any further, she took his hand to lead him back to the dining room. But the moment her fingers came in contact with his, she regretted her offer. Just the casual brush of his flesh against hers made her blood rush. It was stupid to imagine that she could give him a head and neck massage without reacting even more strongly.

But now that she'd been so insistent, how could she back out? He would guess the reason immediately. And, in truth, she really did want to ease his pain. Somehow she would just have to keep her feelings under control.

Doing her best to marshal her wits, she gently pushed him down into the straight chair and then stepped around behind him.

"How is a massage going to help me?" Jim asked, his voice slightly husky. At that moment she knew that he was as affected as she.

"By relaxing you," she answered. "Close your eyes." She pressed her fingertips to his forehead and began to stroke gently outward toward the temples.

Neither of them spoke. Terri had to work hard to control her own breathing to keep it steady and even. She fancied she heard the air hissing softly in and out of her lungs. Or was it Jim's breath she heard? She slipped her fingers to his temples and began rubbing in slow, circular motions. Then she moved down to the pressure point just in front of each ear. As her fingers carried out the massage in a slow, steady rhythm, Jim expelled a ragged breath and let his head sink back slightly against her breast.

"That feels wonderful."

Terri wasn't sure whether he was referring to the soothing motion of her fingers or the contact with her body. But she certainly knew how it was affecting her. As his head brushed the inner sides of her breasts, she felt her nipples tense. Doggedly she tried to ignore the reaction and moved her hands down to the sensitive nerve centers behind his ears.

Under her hands, she felt him shudder slightly. "Am I hurting you?" she asked anxiously.

When he answered, she heard that his voice had deepened several more notes. "Hardly. Actually, I'm beginning to think your brother Tony is a very lucky young man."

Terri thought back to the sisterly relationship she'd always enjoyed with her brother. Touching him was nothing like touching Jim. "Giving Tony a massage never made me feel this way," she thought, and then realized with a little jolt that she'd actually uttered the revealing words.

Under Terri's ministrations, Jim had slumped down into the chair. Now his head jerked up. "And how is that?"

When she didn't answer, he turned and looked up into her downcast face. His eyes were level with her swelling breasts.

Terri could feel the blood warming her cheeks, but still she couldn't find words to answer him.

"If you're not going to say it, then let me," Jim whispered hoarsely. "You might have set out to give me a perfectly innocent massage, but your hands on my skin are

driving me crazy—in the nicest possible way, you understand." As he spoke, he rose to his feet and lifted his arms
as though to pull her close. But after a moment's hesita-
tion, he let them drop to his sides. Terri could see his palms
pressed against the outsides of his pant legs.

"I promised I wouldn't start anything else between the
two of us," he said, looking searchingly into her eyes. "But
in another minute it's going to be impossible to keep that
promise. So I suppose I'd better leave."

Terri's heart seemed to stop and then start up again with
a wrenching lurch. He was perfectly right, and they both
knew it. If she'd wanted to keep things between them pla-
tonic, she never should have invited him here in the first
place. Her second mistake had been to think she could touch
him and not rekindle all the passion that had fired their relationship from the first.

"Maybe that's best," she agreed in a barely audible voice.

Once again, Jim's shoulders seemed to sag slightly. "Yes"
was all he said as he turned to look around for his jacket.
When he found it, he slung it over his shoulder and stood
gazing down at her. "I enjoyed being with you today."

"I enjoyed being with you, too. And thanks. I really ap-
preciated your help. I wouldn't be opening my shop tomorrow if you hadn't helped me stock the shelves."

His dark gaze remained fixed on her face, and a muscle
twitched in his jaw. "I've told you how I feel, Terri. I'm
glad to do anything I can for you."

A moment ago his hands had been clamped to his sides.
Now Terri found her own cold palms pressed to her jean-
clad thighs to keep from reaching out to him. She wanted
more than anything in the world to do that. But a cold little
voice inside her head kept warning her not to be a fool and
open herself up to the kind of vulnerability that had sent her
plummeting into despair only a few days before. Surely it
was wiser to say nothing and let him go.

Yet she couldn't stop a painful lump from forming in her throat as she watched him turn toward the door. When he began to rotate the knob, she clenched her fists and held her breath.

"Good night, Terri," he said as he stepped out onto the landing.

Suddenly there was no way she could force reason to prevail over emotion. "Jim!" she cried as she ran toward him. "Don't go. Stay with me."

He swiveled on his heels. As he stared at her, she saw hope flare in his eyes.

"Do you know what you're saying?"

"Oh, yes," she said, throwing herself into his arms.

"Terri, Terri," he groaned as he embraced her. "I've been so miserable without you." His lips were inches from hers, and he began to kiss her ardently, drawing her up so tightly against himself that her feet barely touched the floor of the landing. His fevered kisses touched on her closed eyelids, her cheeks, her chin. Terri's response was no less passionate.

They were clinging to each other, exchanging kiss for openmouthed kiss, when the door across the way opened with a bang, and one of Terri's neighbors stepped out with a bag full of trash. "Humph," the retired postal worker muttered as he took in the scene before him. Then he stalked toward the stairs.

Terri and Jim looked up in surprise, suddenly aware of their surroundings. Terri knew she should have been mortified, and normally would have been. But when their eyes met, she and Jim both started to laugh.

"Perhaps we'd better step back inside," he growled between chuckles.

Weakly Terri nodded.

When he had pulled her back into her living room and closed the door, he folded her close against his chest again. "Now, where were we?"

Terri looked up at Jim and lifted her arms to lock them around his neck. "Right here," she said, offering him her lips.

He took them, and for long moments they were content to luxuriate in the joy of having come back to each other again. When Jim finally raised his head, there was a question in his eyes. "Does this mean that you've forgiven me, Terri?"

"I—" she began.

But he interrupted her answer with another hard kiss and then whispered urgently, "Please say that it has. I don't think I can go on the way I have—knowing how much I hurt you." There was a pleading expression on his face. As he looked down into her eyes, it changed to something she couldn't read.

"What is it?" she asked.

"I just realized that it's not going to work."

An arrow of ice seemed to dart through Terri's stomach. Her green eyes clouded with confusion, she stared up at Jim. Was he saying that he didn't want her after all?

And then an unthinkable idea struck her. What if all this time he'd just been playing a game to salve his ego? What if he really didn't want her—but had only needed to reassure himself that he could get her back?

Her hands began to tremble. Calling Jim back hadn't been an easy thing to do. Now that she had opened herself up to him again, she didn't know whether she could handle his rejection.

He must have seen on her face some of what was going through her mind.

"Oh, God, Terri," he muttered. "What am I doing to you?" They had been standing awkwardly by the door. With a reassuring squeeze, he took her hand and led her to the sofa. Stiffly she sat down, wondering where this was leading and yet afraid to find out. He settled next to her, careful not to touch her. A frown tugged at his eyebrows as if he was worrying over what he intended to say.

When he finally spoke, it was in a voice brittle with tension. "Terri, a moment ago I realized that I was pressuring you again. What good does it do for you to tell me you forgive me when I've all but forced you into saying it?"

The impact of his words almost robbed her of breath. Unable to speak, she reached for his hand and wove her fingers through his.

He pressed her palm tightly. "I want things to be really right between the two of us this time. I want you so much I can hardly think straight, but I don't want to overwhelm you and have you wonder tomorrow morning what it meant."

Still unable to respond, Terri worried her bottom lip between her teeth.

Seeing the look on her face, Jim drew her close and settled her face against his chest, stroking his fingers across her cheek and combing them through her hair.

She relaxed against him, listening to the accelerated thump of his heart. Its frantic rhythm told her more explicitly than words that despite his outward control, he was far from being as calm as he sounded. He continued to run his fingers through her hair. "I'm petrified, you know," he ventured.

"Petrified?"

"Yes. It's been a long time since I let anybody into the citadel I've constructed for myself."

In answer, she pressed more tightly against him.

He cleared his throat. "Maybe the problem is that I had a good marriage. After my wife died, I convinced myself that I just wasn't going to find another woman I wanted to spend my life with."

Terri held her breath, wondering what Jim was about to say.

Gently he tipped her face up to his. "Then I met you."

His warm words had melted the arrow of ice. "Oh, Jim."

"Terri, at this moment I want you very much. But I also want you to know that it isn't just physical with me. I think the two of us could build something very special together. I sensed that back at Hearthwood. In fact, that night after we watched the movie and ended up almost becoming lovers, I was afraid you might try to slip away from me. So I went back to my room and called the desk clerk. What I did was trick him into telling me your last name."

So that was when he'd found out who she was, Terri thought.

"Before I left my office, I'd read your letter so I recognized your name. I knew I had to tell you the next morning who I was. And believe me, Terri, I tried."

She nodded. "Yes, I remember how scathing I was at breakfast about T. & H."

His fingers tightened on her shoulders. "I was afraid to take the chance of losing you before we got to know each other. That's why I was too cowardly to tell you who I was. And, God help me, I was arrogant enough to think that once we'd made love, you would be mine and somehow everything would be all right."

Terri opened her mouth to speak, but Jim laid a finger across her lips. "Let me finish this rather painful confession while I can. I woke up that morning, found you gone and realized what an idiotic mistake I'd made. And I've been trying ever since to get you back." He sighed. "I'm praying that things are different now. Neither of us has any secrets from the other, and I'm no longer dumb enough to think that making love with you is the solution to all our problems. So, if you have any lingering doubts about our being together tonight, tell me now. Because what I want between the two of us is honesty."

Terri gazed up at him, amazed and moved by the way his confession had laid bare his innermost feeling—and by the sincerity she read in his eyes. He hadn't exactly said he loved her, but he'd come very close. And at that moment she began to wonder if she didn't love him. She didn't know what love was. All she knew was that her feelings for Jim were stronger than what she'd ever felt for any other man. And she wanted him—wanted him desperately.

"Jim, right now I feel like getting up and bolting the door to make sure you can't leave."

His laugh was edged with relief and gladness.

"The only thing that worries me," Terri continued, "is that I forgot to make my bed this morning, and I'm afraid you'll think I'm a terrible housekeeper."

He laughed again, and the lines of strain that had been puckering his brow vanished, to be replaced by a different sort of intensity. "Believe me, I'm going to be focused on you, not the bedroom."

He tenderly cupped her face with his hands, and his passionate kiss convinced her that he'd spoken the truth. He stood up, reached for her elbows and with effortless strength lifted her to her feet. "Let's go take a look at this unmade bed of yours," he suggested huskily.

Terri nodded. Arm in arm, they made their way down the hall.

Terri had always considered her bedroom her private retreat, and she'd decorated it to please herself. Her brass bed had a bright red and blue cover and pillow shams. The matchstick blinds at her windows were blue, as were the soft swags that framed them. The rest of the furniture was Victorian. Terri had inherited the marble-topped bureau, dresser and rocking chair from her aunt and refinished them herself.

Despite his disclaimer, Jim paused in the doorway to look around. "I like it very much, and I think you should keep your bed unmade. Those flowered sheets are very inviting." He turned to Terri and folded her into his arms. As he pulled her close, she realized that what he'd said in the living room made a tremendous difference to how she felt now.

Eagerly she returned his kiss. Craving even more contact, she slipped her hands under the hem of his sweater and reached up to stroke the warm flesh of his back.

"Nice," he murmured, the words a warm, thrilling caress against her neck.

"Better than the massage I gave you earlier?"

She felt an answering rumble in his chest before he spoke. "It's all relative. What you were doing to my head and neck was wonderful. But with those talented hands under my sweater, there's a certain anticipation of even more delights."

It was the same for Terri. Now that she and Jim were sure of each other's intentions, it was a joy to draw out that sweetness.

Playfully he toyed with the buttons on her blouse. "I don't think you really need this, do you?" he questioned as he began to slowly undo them.

"Only to keep warm," she teased.

"Don't worry. I intend to keep you very warm."

Her answer was a little gasp as he lowered his head and flicked out his tongue to stroke the sensitive valley that he had just uncovered.

While his mouth lingered on her flesh, he moved his hands around to her back, and she felt his fingers slip beneath the elastic where her bra was hooked. Terri held her breath, expecting him to open it at any moment. Instead, he simply stroked her back as he turned his face from side to side, nuzzling the lace-sheathed mounds of her breasts. Terri felt them swell in response, her nipples tightening with excitement. Suddenly she longed to feel Jim's mouth against her bare flesh. But he didn't unhook her bra. When she realized he was going to make her wait, she moaned with frustration.

"What is it? What do you want?" he asked quickly. But denying her was also denying himself, and suddenly he couldn't wait any longer to taste her sweetness.

With shaking fingers, he snapped open the hook and pushed her bra and her open blouse from her shoulders. Then he was lifting her breasts in his hands, so that his lips and tongue could ravish first one and then the other.

The pleasure of his mouth on her sensitized skin was so intense that Terri's legs seemed to melt beneath her, and she sagged toward him.

With a groan he lifted Terri into his arms and carried her toward the bed. After lowering her onto the sheets, he stood for an electric moment looking down at her half-naked body. Then he yanked his own sweater over his head, baring his broad, furred chest.

When Terri saw him begin to unbuckle his leather belt, the muscles in her stomach tightened. She fumbled frantically at the snap on her jeans. In the next moment he was naked and kneeling over her on the bed. Terri had wriggled out of her jeans and was reaching up to rid herself of her panties when Jim's hands covered hers.

"Let me do that," he said hoarsely.

Her eyes locked with his and she watched as he lowered his head to the soft curve of her bared belly. Sensuously he kissed the skin at the top of her panties. Then, just as he had run his finger under the closure of her bra, he flicked his tongue beneath the softly elasticized lace. Terri shuddered with excitement.

"I've lain awake at night wondering if I'd ever be with you like this again." His voice grated as he slipped his fingers under the silky fabric. For a moment he caressed the triangle of soft curly hair at the juncture of her legs. Then he slid his hand lower.

It was impossible for Terri to keep still. Her body twisted urgently against his relentless fingers, and her hands clenched on his shoulder.

"Jim, please don't make me wait any longer," she implored.

But Jim had reached the breaking point, too. In one fluid motion he stripped the panties away and covered her writhing body with his own.

Their lovemaking had been urgent before. Now it was explosively passionate. For Terri there had never been such rapture in surrender. And as Jim conquered her, he was himself enslaved. They moved together as one, and when the earth-shattering climax seized them, they clung to each other like halves of the same whole.

"Oh, Terri, I love you so much!" Jim cried.

It was a moment before she was able to take in his words. When she did, her eyes flew open. Had she heard him right? she wondered. But it was not something she could ask. And when his mouth covered hers again, there was no further thought of questions.

Ten

I'd like to spend the night with you—but we both have to get to work early in the morning," Jim said.

Terri snuggled against his warmth, torn between practicality and what she really wanted.

"What I'd like best of all is to ask you to move in with me," he continued, watching her closely. When he saw the panicked expression on her face, he added quickly, "But I know I'd be pushing you. And besides, it would be an awfully long commute for you from my place to Sommerset Mall."

Terri angled her head up so that she could look at him. He was right. It had been a long time since she'd thought of herself as being anywhere but on her own. Although her feelings for Jim were very strong, she really needed time to get used to the idea of the two of them being a couple.

He reached out to stroke his thumb across her lips. "I won't ask you to say anything now. But I do want to stay here with you for a while longer."

"I'd like that, too." Maybe she wasn't ready yet to talk about the future, but after their sweet lovemaking, she hated to think that he was going and wanted to savor his closeness.

Terri rested her head on Jim's shoulder. She had no doubts that what had just happened between them was right. But she'd struggled so hard to take charge of her life, and things were moving so fast now. Jim's natural assertiveness was a little alarming. And she couldn't help remembering why she'd broken off her youthful engagement.

Jim was quick to sense her mood. "Is something wrong?" he asked gently.

"Only that I feel a bit overwhelmed."

"Overwhelmed in the right way, I hope."

"Mmm-hmm," Terri murmured against his shoulder. Now that their passion was spent, she couldn't help noticing that Jim's voice sounded tired. And she thought again about the long hours he'd spent getting her shop ready to open.

"I guess it wasn't your usual kind of weekend," she ventured.

"It was one of the best weekends of my life!" He pulled her back down beside him and settled the covers around them once more.

Sometime after midnight, Jim regretfully climbed out of bed. "I'll call you tomorrow to see how things are going," he promised.

She could imagine how busy he was going to be Monday morning. "You don't have to do that. Why don't you wait until we both get home?"

"All right," he said, then kissed her tenderly.

When he was finally gone, she lay back in her silent bedroom and looked through the moonlit shadows at the familiar surroundings. Again she remembered Jim's declaration. Had he really said he loved her? Before they'd made love, he'd as much as said he wanted a long-term relationship. And then he'd mentioned the possibility of their living together. The thought was exhilarating, but also rather frightening. She'd never thought about what it would take to make a loving partnership work. Whatever it was, she found herself daring to hope that she and Jim had it.

Terri was still pondering the question the next morning as she pulled into the parking lot of Sommerset Mall.

The mall wouldn't open for over an hour, but there were still a few things she hadn't yet attended to. After letting herself in through the back door of her shop, Terri threaded her way through the jumbled stockroom. It really was a mess. And as soon as she had the time, she would straighten it up. But it couldn't be her first priority—particularly when she was going to have to be out front most of the time, waiting on customers.

Terri spent the time remaining before the store opened putting out a few things they hadn't gotten to the day before. Just before ten o'clock, a delivery boy tapped at the front door. He was holding a magnificent flower arrangement in a wide crystal bowl.

"Are you sure you have the right place?" Terri asked in amazement.

He glanced at the form in his hand. "If you're Terri Genetti, these are for you."

She accepted the fragrant offering and looked admiringly at the red roses set off with baby's breath. They would go perfectly with the color scheme of her bedroom, she thought, and knew who must have sent them.

In fact, the card attached to the arrangement was from Jim. "Thinking of you," it read.

Smiling, Terri set the thoughtful present on the counter. She was standing back to admire it when the bell over the door jangled and her first customer came in.

It was a woman who had been a regular patron since Terri had initially opened at Sommerset Mall.

"I'm so glad you're back in business," she gushed. "I was out of that cinnamon tea I like to drink, and I didn't know where else to get it."

"Well, it's right over here on the shelf," Terri directed her. "You can count on finding it in stock at Gourmet Galore."

The woman bought three boxes of tea and some of the new preserves Terri had decided to try. Almost as soon as she had left the store, another customer arrived and then another. In fact, it was a successful morning.

When Bonnie stopped by at noon to see how things were going, she had to wait while Terri rang up several more sales.

"Well, it looks as though business is booming," she commented.

Terri grinned. "Pretty good so far."

Bonnie spied the flowers on the counter. "The mall mangement didn't send you those, did they?"

"In a manner of speaking. They're from Jim."

"But I can't believe they have anything to do with business," Bonnie teased. "You can tell me all about it over lunch—which I'll go out and bring back. What do you say to my picking us up a couple of Greek salads from the new place down by the fountain?"

"Sounds delicious. That's exactly what I'm in the mood to eat," Terri told her gratefully.

But Bonnie had no sooner turned toward the door than another delivery boy appeared. This time the young man was carrying a large paper bag.

"I have a lunch order for Terri Genetti," he declared.

Bonnie raised an eyebrow. "Why didn't you tell me you'd already sent out for something?"

"I didn't." A puzzled expression wrinkling her brow, Terri turned toward the young man. "Who sent this?"

He pulled a sheaf of order forms from his pocket and riffled through them. "A Mr. Holbrook."

"Oh, I see," Bonnie said.

Terri accepted the bag. After the boy had turned to leave, she peered inside. There were at least five neatly wrapped sandwiches along with several pieces of fruit and some soft drinks.

Bonnie looked over her friend's shoulder. "I guess he's not taking a chance on your wasting away. Very flattering."

"Yes," Terri said, and she was flattered. She also felt a bit quizzical. Did Jim think she wasn't sensible enough to stop for lunch?

"Well, I guess I don't have to go out and get salads," Bonnie observed. "There's enough in that bag to feed an army." As she spoke, she began to take out the sandwiches. "Quite a selection, too. Egg salad. Ham and cheese. Roast beef. Tuna. What's your pleasure?"

Terri looked at the array. Actually she wasn't in the mood for a sandwich. She'd had her taste buds all set for the Greek salad. On the other hand, it was ridiculous to waste good food.

"We could each have half the tuna and half the egg salad," Bonnie suggested.

"That's fine."

The conversation was interrupted by the arrival of another customer. When the man had left, Bonnie sat down on the bench against the wall. "Something you can hold in your hand and put down quickly is really more practical than a salad—if you're going to have to wait on customers while you eat."

Terri nodded.

"When are you planning to hire some help?" Bonnie asked.

Terri unwrapped the two sandwiches and handed half of each to her friend. "That's next on my agenda."

After a few bites of the tuna fish, Bonnie looked across at her friend. "If this lunch is any indication, I'd say that you and Jim Holbrook are back on good terms."

Terri thoughtfully chewed some egg salad before answering. "Yes, we are."

Bonnie took another bite, then licked her lips. "This is a terrific sandwich. He certainly knows how to take care of his friends."

"I don't believe he made it himself," Terri shot back.

Bonnie laughed. "Surely you don't think that's what I meant? Listen, don't you know a good thing when it comes up and grabs you by the ankle, Terri? This guy's got to be one in a million."

"Yes, he is," Terri admitted. "But in a way that's sort of got me worried."

"What do you mean? As far as I'm concerned, you can't have too much of a good thing."

Terri struggled to express what she was feeling. "It's just that Jim Holbrook is really a rather overpowering man, and I'm used to doing things for myself. You know, I really would rather have had the salad you were going to pick up than his sandwiches."

Bonnie looked amazed. "But that's silly. How can you object to being well taken care of?"

"Haven't you ever heard about the bird in the gilded cage?" Terri retorted. "Don't you remember my telling you that I once broke off an engagement because I was afraid that was going to happen to me?"

"But that guy was a male chauvinist," Bonnie protested. "And Jim Holbrook doesn't seem to be anything like that. I'd call him a fantastic guy."

"So would I," Terri agreed. She knew her friend was right. She really was overreacting to what anyone else would consider a thoughtful gesture.

That evening when Jim called, she thanked him warmly for the lunch and the beautiful flowers.

"I wanted you to know I was thinking about you," he returned. "What I really wish is that I could take you out to dinner this evening. But I guess you're beat."

"Yes, I am."

"Well, tell me about your day."

Terri obliged enthusiastically.

"It sounds as though things are going great," Jim said approvingly. "But you can't handle all that business by yourself. You need to get someone to help out."

"I realize that."

Jim wasn't willing to let the matter drop. "I don't like to think about your wearing yourself out. Let's talk about it some more tomorrow night."

"I think we have more interesting things to discuss than business problems," Terri replied. She was beginning to feel slightly pressed. Why wouldn't Jim simply accept her judgment on this?

He laughed. "Maybe you're right. I was hoping we could get together Wednesday."

"I'd like that." And she knew as she spoke the words that they were true. Even though it had been less than twenty-four hours since Jim had left her and she'd had an exhausting day, the thought of being in his arms again was like a dose of strong stimulant.

He caught the change in her voice and said in a low, intimate tone, "Does that mean you'd like me to come over tonight?"

After a brief struggle with herself, Terri let reason prevail. "I would. But I really do need a full night's sleep. And so do you."

"You're right. But I wish you weren't," Jim agreed.

Still, neither of them wanted to end the call, and they talked until Terri couldn't suppress a yawn.

"Is that what I do to you, put you to sleep?" Jim joked.

"Of course not. It's from getting hardly any rest—and then being on my feet for twelve hours straight."

"Well, perhaps I can't do anything about your feet, but I do apologize for keeping you up so late last night."

"Don't apologize. Last night was wonderful."

They chatted for a few more minutes. When Terri hung up, she was smiling—and looking forward to Wednesday. But before that she had to get through Tuesday.

The next morning was much like the one before, satisfyingly busy. She and Bonnie were just discussing what they might like for lunch, when another catered repast arrived from Jim.

"Really, you can't complain," Bonnie observed. "This time he's even sent shrimp salad—my favorite."

"Well, it's not mine," Terri said. "I was in the mood for soup."

Bonnie poked in the bottom of the bag. "That's here, too. There's a carton of chicken noodle. It's almost as good as having a Jewish mother."

Terri didn't reply. But she knew that when Jim called that night, she was going to tell him to stop being so overprotective.

She had even more reason to be flabbergasted by his solicitude that afternoon when a tall blond boy walked into the shop. "Hi. I'm Ted Ross. They said over at the mall office that I was to come over and help you out."

Terri's mouth dropped open. "What are you talking about?"

After he repeated himself, Terri shook her head. "I'm sorry if they misled you. But I can't afford to take on extra help at this time. Maybe a little closer to Christmas."

"Oh, I don't think you understand," Ted replied. "The mall is paying for twenty hours a week of my time."

Terri digested this startling piece of news in silence. Then she turned toward the phone. "Just give me a moment while I check on this."

Dave Patterson, the mall manager, answered her question cheerfully. "Why, yes, Ms. Genetti. Mr. Holbrook called us this morning and made the arrangements. We have money set aside for a youth incentive program, and he asked that one of the applicants be assigned to you."

"Isn't that rather unusual?" Terri inquired.

"Yes. But Mr. Holbrook seems to be taking a special interest in your shop."

Terri could hardly repress her chagrin. From his tone of voice it was obvious that Mr. Patterson thought she was having an affair with Jim Holbrook—and added his own interpretation. She could just imagine him thinking she had traded sexual favors to get her store back. And Jim's overprotective behavior was lending credence to that notion. For someone as proud as Terri, that was hard to take. "I see," she said in a clipped voice. "And what would happen if I sent Ted Ross back to you to be assigned elsewhere?"

"He wouldn't have a job, since all our regular positions are filled."

"Thank you for enlightening me," Terri replied before hanging up. She turned back to Ted to find him looking at her expectantly. Her first impulse was still to tell him that she didn't need his help. But that hardly seemed fair to the young man, since he had nothing to do with all this.

"Do you have any retail experience?" she asked.

"Yes. I worked in one of the mall clothing stores all summer."

Well, at least he knew how to operate a cash register and process credit cards. Maybe she could let him mind the front of the shop while she did some sorting out in the back. When she had things straightened out a bit, they could switch places.

Ted stayed till closing time, and Terri was pleased with his performance. But that didn't stop a knot of tension from forming in her chest when she thought about the high-handed way in which Jim seemed to be interfering in her life. She knew his intentions were good, and it was hard to be angry with someone who was trying to do her a favor. Still, her stomach churned as she glanced through the stockroom doorway and saw Ted standing at the counter.

When Terri got home, she drew a hot bath, stripped off her work clothes and settled gratefully into the soothing warmth. She was just massaging her aching insteps when the phone rang. What timing! she thought, shutting her eyes as though that would block out the noise. Maybe she'd just let it ring until whoever it was gave up and called back later. But the person on the other end of the line—and she was beginning to suspect she knew who it was—apparently wasn't willing to take no for an answer. Finally, rolling her eyes with exasperation and envying people who could afford answering machines, she hauled herself out of the tub. Wrapping her dripping body in a towel, she made a trail of wet footprints down the hall to the phone.

"Did you just walk in the door?" Jim asked

"No, I was in the tub."

"Oh, then I'm sorry I got you out," he responded. "But I was worried when you didn't answer."

"Jim, I've been taking care of myself for years. You needn't worry about me."

"I can't help myself," Jim said cheerfully. "You're a very special lady, and I'm feeling all sorts of protective urges toward you. As well as certain others," he added. "I can't wait until tomorrow night."

Terri looked down to see the pool of water at her feet. Bending over, she dabbed at her legs to stanch the rivulets that were tracking down her calves.

"I'm looking forward to it, too," she told Jim. "But there is something I want to discuss with you. That boy you sent over to my shop."

"They said he was well recommended. How's he working out?"

Terri brushed wet hair out of her eyes and searched for the right words. "He's very good. But you shouldn't be doing me all these special favors."

"I was doing Ted more of a favor than I was you. According to Dave Patterson, he needed the job to make up next semester's tuition."

"Oh."

How could she argue with that? Terri wondered. Yet she made a stab at it. "You remember when we talked about my needing to feel independent? Well, how can I feel that way when someone else is paying my employee's salary?"

"Terri, you're too sensitive. In my experience, most women like to be taken care of."

What experience was that? Terri asked herself. Was he referring to his wife—or to a string of girlfriends?

On the other end of the line he chuckled. "I was sending sandwiches and a stock boy, not diamonds and mink—which is, by the way, really what I'd like to be showering you with," he added warmly. "But I wouldn't want you to feel like somebody's mistress."

Terri shivered in her towel. Unfortunately, that was part of the problem. "You didn't hear Patterson's voice when he told me you had taken a special interest in my shop. Jim, a kept woman was exactly what I felt like."

Jim's voice became gruff. "Well, I'll certainly make sure that doesn't happen again."

"Please don't say anything to him," she begged. "I'd be mortified."

It took some arguing, but Jim finally agreed to let the matter drop.

Terri hesitated for a moment and then decided that it was better to get everything that was bothering her off her chest. "And please,"she went on, "don't go to the trouble of sending lunch again."

"That's not much trouble. When I order my own, I have my secretary put in an extra order for yours."

So his secretary was in on their secret, too, she thought, her face growing hot. Why didn't he just take an ad out in the *Washington Post*? "Well, please don't," she said more

harply than she meant to. "Now that I have some help, I'd
ike to go out for lunch."

"Yes, it's probably good for you to have a change of
cene. I worry about you being in that little store all day."

Little store, Terri thought. That place had been her life for
he past three years. Making a success of it was as impor-
ant to her as making a success of T. & H. was to Jim. But
he didn't want to get into an argument with him, so she let
he subject drop.

After they'd set the time for Wednesday's dinner, Terri
eturned to the bathroom. But the water in the tub was now
nly lukewarm and had lost its appeal. So she pulled the
lug, finished drying herself off and slipped into a cozy
obe. She was just taking one of her quick breads out of the
reezer to heat it up for a simple dinner, when the phone
ang again.

After sticking her slice of bread into the toaster oven, she
icked up the receiver.

The voice on the other end of the line made her face light
p. It was her brother Tony.

"Are you back in town?" she exclaimed.

"Yup. I finally shook Florida off my heels."

They chatted for a few minutes about his recent adven-
ures, and she filled him in on the family news. Finally he
leared his throat. "Sis, you sound nice and friendly. I
asn't so sure of the reception you were going to give me
fter I turned you down on that loan."

Terri smiled at the receiver. "In the first place, you're my
avorite brother. And in the second, I knew you would have
nt me the money if you'd had it."

His voice had grown serious. "Yes, I would have. How
re things going with the shop? Do you still need cash?"

"I got a loan."

"That's too bad."

"Too bad?"

"Yes, I had a bit of luck in a billiard tournament down in Miami."

"Luck. You mean skill."

He laughed. "Well, whatever—it was very profitable."

If only this had happened a week ago, Terri thought.

"I was hoping you'd let me invest some of the cash before it slips through my fingers," her brother continued.

"Really?" Terri lifted her brows thoughtfully. Tony wasn't kidding about his attitude toward money. With him it was either boom or bust, and she'd often worried about how he would eventually take care of himself. It would be good for him to invest in something more stable than fast women and flashy clothes. Aloud she said, "The paper work hasn't been finished on the loan yet. Maybe we should discuss what amount you were thinking about investing."

Tony named a figure that made her eyes widen. He really must have done well.

"If you went in with me, it would have to be a long-term investment," Terri cautioned. As she spoke, she wedged the receiver between her ear and her shoulder and opened the toaster oven to take out her bread.

"That's exactly what I'm looking for," he assured her. "So far, my attitude toward everything—especially money—has been too short-term. And I have faith in you, kid."

"When can we get together and talk about specifics?" Terri asked.

"How about tomorrow night?"

She shook her head. As anxious as she was to see her brother, she wasn't going to cancel out on Jim. "Not tomorrow. I have a dinner date."

"Hey, that's great. Anybody I know?"

"No. But he's someone you'd like."

"Then I'll look forward to meeting him."

After they'd arranged to meet on Thursday night, Terri hung up. For a moment she sat by the phone, staring to ward the darkened window. This was a completely unexpected development—but one that, the more she thought about it, opened up all kinds of welcome possibilities.

Meditatively she took a bite of her oven-warmed banana bread. As she savored the delicate flavor, she smiled. Tony's money might be the solution to her problem.

She wanted to be an equal in what was developing between Jim and herself. And how could she achieve that when she was at his mercy as far as her livelihood was concerned? If she canceled the loan he was personally arranging, she'd feel better about their relationship, because they'd no longer be mixing two aspects of her life that she wanted to keep separate.

But how would he feel about that? As Terri munched on, she thought about Jim's overprotective behavior since she'd agreed to let him take her under his wing. He might see her decision as a slap in the face. She was going to have to broach this new development to him carefully, if she didn't want him to see it as some sort of rejection.

Eleven

Much as Terri loved being in her new shop, Wednesday
seemed to drag. She was impatient, not only because she
couldn't wait to spend the evening with Jim but also because she wanted to get things between them straightened
out. When she opened the door to him that night, a warm
smile lit her face.

"Well, this is quite a welcome. You must have had a good
day in the store." He grinned mischievously. "Or dare I
hope that seeing me again makes you look as though you've
just won the lottery?"

"Both," Terri told him. "But especially seeing you." As
she spoke, she took in his appearance. Instead of his usual
business suit, he was dressed in a closely woven blue and
white striped oxford cloth shirt, khaki trousers and a handsome heather tweed sport coat. On Jim the combination was
devastating.

When he held out his arms, she flew into them eagerly.

"It's so good to hold you after so long," he declared.

Terri understood exactly what he meant. They had been separated for only a few days, but it felt like an eternity. He lowered his head, and they savored each other's lips for long moments.

"What's that wonderful fragrance I'm smelling?" he finally whispered against her ear.

She chuckled. "It's either my new perfume or the beef Burgundy warming in the oven."

"Beef Burgundy? Don't tell me you rushed home to cook a fancy dinner," Jim said, stroking her back and nuzzling his face against her neck.

Shaking her head, she pulled away gently. "I'm tempted to lie, but the truth is I took advantage of a catering shop on my way home."

Jim looked quizzical. "When I asked you to have dinner with me, I thought we were going out."

"You're always doing things for me. Let me return the favor."

"Fair enough."

Well, that was a good beginning, Terri thought. All day she'd been mulling over Tony's offer and what it would mean to her budding relationship with Jim. So she'd planned a special evening to put him in the right mood before telling him about it.

In addition to the delicious meal that was warming in the oven, she'd taken extra care with her appearance. She was wearing a long, flowered hostess gown that she rarely took out of the closet but had seemed just the thing for tonight. It clung to her curves and swept her feet in a swirl of soft emerald-green silk.

"That gown does wonderful things for your beautiful eyes—not to mention your gorgeous body," Jim murmured as his gaze swept over her. "I don't think I've ever seen you looking more beautiful, and that's saying something—since I thought you were stunning the first time I laid eyes on you."

Terri's face lit up. "Flattery will get you everywhere—but not until you've had a drink and eaten dinner."

"That sounds promising." As he stepped into the room, Jim set a manila folder on the coffee table.

Terri glanced at it. "What's that?"

"Oh, just a little something I worked up for you. We'll talk about it later."

For a moment Terri frowned. Trust Jim to try to steer the evening in a direction she hadn't counted on. But she wasn't going to let things get too far off track.

Instead of asking him questions about the mysterious folder, she poured them each a glass of red wine and led him to the candle-lit table.

The meal was everything she had hoped it would be. Jim seemed to relish not only the good food but also the romantic atmosphere she'd created.

She'd planned an amaretto cheesecake for dessert. But as she got up to take the dinner plates to the kitchen, Jim stood, too. He gave her time enough only to set the dishes on the counter before turning her around and drawing her into his arms.

"If you were out to seduce me this evening, you certainly succeeded," he whispered roughly. "I think I'll have my dessert in the bedroom."

As Terri looked up into the passion-dark pools of his eyes, she forgot all about the amaretto cheesecake and melted helplessly against him. A moment later Jim's mouth found hers, while a hand went to the front zipper on her long emerald gown.

"I knew you weren't wearing a bra under that sexy silk," he muttered. "And thinking about it has been driving me around the bend."

Jim's obvious impatience was incredibly arousing. As the gown slithered to the floor and he caught her up in his arms and began to carry her down the hall, Terri clung to him, shivering with impatience.

In the darkened cocoon of her small bedroom they took shelter in each other's desire. It had always been difficult for Terri to come to terms with the blinding passion this man aroused in her. Yet in the circle of his embrace, she found what she longed for.

As their lips fused and their hands roused each other to fever pitch, she wanted to give and give and give. And his passionate yet tender attentions told her that his goals were identical. Magically, by giving everything they could, each received more than seemed humanly possible.

A long time later, they lay utterly satisfied in each other's arms. Floating in a sea of contentment, her eyes closed, Terri drew one hand across Jim's broad, hair-thatched chest.

"You know," she said dreamily, "I spent a long time planning this dinner."

"Mmm."

"And after you'd eaten it and were in a good mood, there was something I wanted to discuss with you."

Lazily he stroked the satin skin of her shoulder. "Well, I couldn't possibly be in a better mood than I am now." He sounded every bit as serene as a man ought who'd eaten a delicious meal and then made love. He continued to cuddle her and then turned his head so that his lips could play with the edge of her ear. "Is what you want to talk about business or pleasure?"

"Business, I'm afraid," Terri admitted, giggling and drawing back as he nipped gently at her tender flesh.

"Well, in that case, I have something I want to talk to you about, too. It won't take long, so why don't we go out into the kitchen and discuss it over that dessert we never got around to eating?"

Somewhat quizzically, Terri agreed. A few minutes later she, clad in a robe, and Jim, in his shirt and slacks, went back to the kitchen, where she sliced them each a piece of cheesecake.

"Why don't you let me go first?" Jim suggested. "This will be the first time I've discussed inventory control while eating cheesecake with a woman in a bathrobe."

Terri wrinkled her brow. "Inventory control?"

"Yes," he said cheerfully. "I've been thinking about the mess in your stockroom, and I've come up with something that might interest you. Don't get up. I'll be right back."

Terri blinked as he pushed back his chair and disappeared into the living room. He reappeared in a moment, holding the folder she'd seen him set on the table earlier.

Smiling at Terri, he withdrew several sheets of paper, which he handed to her with a flourish. "Maybe this isn't quite the time, but when you have a minute, you might want to study these. I think you'll find that this system will really make short work of your chaotic storage problem."

When he'd walked out of the kitchen, Terri had still been trying to figure out what he was up to. Now her jaw dropped open as Jim placed a set of complicated-looking instructions on the table in front of her. A moment ago she'd been feeling wonderfully peaceful. Now, as she stared down at the directions written in a forceful male hand, her stomach began to churn. The details swam before her eyes. Terri put the papers down, hugged her robe around her and gave the man she'd just made love with a direct look. "Jim, I'm afraid I'm not up to absorbing something as complicated as this right now. And even if I were, I'd rather just go on my instincts. That's the way I've always done it."

"Sweetheart," Jim said gently, reaching out to caress her shoulder, "your instincts are terrific. But in today's cutthroat business world, that's just not enough. Take my word for it—you need to be more analytical."

Terri's eyes narrowed, and she clenched her hands on the robe. But she still tried to sound calm. Perhaps he was right. However, all she knew at the moment was that she couldn' cope with any more of his well-meaning interference. " appreciate your help," she told him. "You've obviously gone to a lot of trouble to work this up for me. But Gourmet Galore is my store, and it's important that I do things my way. I thought you understood that. Back at Hearthwood, I told you how much I needed to feel independent. My family doesn't think that a woman alone can make it, and I need to prove to them—and to myself—that I can."

Jim pushed back his plate and steepled his hands in front of him on the table. "I know you have this fixation about doing everything your way. But we're really talking about the same thing. You did tell me about your family and how you were always the last in line, so I understand why it's very important to you to succeed right now. All I'm trying to do is give you every chance to make it."

Terri was so upset that she ignored his conciliatory tone and heard his last sentence as an attack on her business acumen. "But don't you see? You're not letting me make my own decisions," she flared. "You've already picked my staff, instead of allowing me to do my own interviewing. I was going to get somebody next week, and it would have been a woman—with experience in the food business."

He tried to interrupt, but she plowed on. "And you won't even do me the courtesy of letting me decide what I want for lunch."

Jim frowned. "I don't mean to smother you—or pull rank. Maybe I just care about you too much."

Terri could feel a pulse pounding in her temples. Although she fought to rein in her emotions and not say anything she would regret later, she could no longer control her tongue. "Are you sure it's me you care about and not your reputation as the business whiz who never makes a bad decision?"

Jim's mouth tightened. How could she say that to him, when he'd been jumping through hoops to get back in her good graces? He was so anxious for her to succeed that he'd even spent hours helping her arrange her shelves—time he couldn't afford. And the job would have been a damn sight easier if her stockroom hadn't looked like the aftermath of a tornado. That's why he'd been up almost all of Tuesday night, working on this damn system. "Of course not," he said in as controlled a tone as he could manage. "But since you brought the subject up, the loan my company is making you *is* my responsibility. And I do have a perfect right to—"

Terri yanked the lapels of her robe even tighter, and her green eyes glittered dangerously. "Well, perhaps I can relieve you of that millstone," she interrupted sharply. "As it happens, I don't need your loan anymore."

Jim stared at her as if he were a tax auditor and she'd just told him she'd falsified her returns for the past ten years. *"What?"*

"You heard me," Terri said with all the dignity she could muster. "I don't want your money, and I don't need it."

"That's not what you told me four days ago. Do you realize what I've had to go through to make this loan to you? You're not exactly the best risk in town, you know," he reminded her sardonically.

"Then why did you offer?" As she spoke, Terri stood up and drew the belt on her robe so tight that the cord cut into her waist.

"Because I wanted to help you and because I thought you deserved that help," Jim said, also pushing back his chair. As he stood, he began to button his shirt. "But if you have so little trust in my motives, perhaps you're not the woman I wanted to believe you were." The flat statement and the way he made it almost took her breath away.

"I think you'd better leave." There was no force to her words; they came out like a thin gasp.

"Well, at least we can agree on something. That's exactly what I'm going to do." He started toward the living room, realized he was barefoot and backtracked down the hall to the bedroom.

Not quite knowing why, Terri followed and forced herself to watch as he yanked the rest of his clothes on. Ignoring her, he finished and stalked to the door. But just before he reached it, he whirled and gave her a look that froze the blood in her veins. "You realize that after all the paperwork that's been done to process your loan, there will be a five percent penalty for withdrawing the application. Am I going to pay it, or are you?"

Unshed tears burned in her eyes, but she was damned if she was going to let him see her break down. "I wouldn't dream of taking the money from you!" she managed to say.

"You were certainly willing to take money from me when you were desperate," he shot back. "Would you mind satisfying my curiosity about where your unexpected pot of gold has come from?"

"My brother."

"Oh" was all Jim said, but Terri suspected from the dark expression on his face that he didn't believe her. The thought made her so furious that for a moment she lost control completely. As Jim strode down the hall, she picked up one of her shoes and hurled it after him. It just missed him, clunking against a wall.

At that, her hand went to her mouth, and she pressed her fingers hard against her lips to keep from crying out herself.

Jim didn't turn or even break his stride. A moment later he closed her front door very softly behind him and was gone.

The click of the latch was a very final sound. Suddenly Terri found that it was no longer possible to hold back the tears that had been threatening to overwhelm her. Misery overtook her in a great rush, and her legs couldn't support her weight. She sank onto the bed, but it was too much of an effort even to sit up. Flopping over, she rolled to one side, pulled up her knees and buried her face in the sheets, which were still warm.

At first her sobs were long and racking, and she could do nothing but yield to mindless heartache. Yet it was possible to cry for only so long. Inevitably and painfully, the well of her tears ran dry. As her mind began to function again, she sat up and looked toward the doorway through which Jim had disappeared. She'd been looking forward so much to seeing him again. She'd had such positive feelings about tonight! The evening had even started off just the way she had anticipated. How had things gone wrong so quickly? But she knew the answer to that. It had been the combination of Jim's drive to solve what he saw as her problems and her own stubborn pride.

She clenched her fists and pressed them against her eyes as if to blot out the picture of her beloved store that had suddenly formed in her mind. And why had her pride in it—in her self-sufficiency—become such an issue? The answer made her draw in a deep, shuddering breath.

There was something she hadn't allowed herself to fully acknowledge until this moment: now something else in her life was just as important as—no, more important than—what the store symbolized. She loved Jim Holbrook. Probably she'd loved him ever since Hearthwood. But she'd been unable to admit it to herself because of the same pride that had made her lash out at him just now. What had really been bothering her all week was not so much his over-protectiveness—which was really very flattering, she silently admitted now. It had, however, only underlined her own feelings of inadequacy. She'd worked so hard to be independent. And if she was going to give that up, she needed to go as an equal to the man she loved.

In love with Jim! The thought brought a burgeoning, swelling feeling to her heart. She'd imagined once before that she'd been in love, but the emotions she'd experienced then paled by comparison to what she felt now. Closing her eyes, she remembered the exquisite joy she'd found in his embrace. He'd brought her to the heights of passion but also shown her the real meaning of security. If only he were here now, holding her, telling her that they belonged to each other and that everything was going to be all right. But she was too honest to deceive herself. After her award-winning performance tonight, she could imagine that Jim Holbrook wasn't going to want her on any terms.

The realization brought a fresh and even more painful lump to her throat. She struggled to get a grip on her runaway anguish, yet even though she squeezed her eyes shut, she couldn't prevent more tears from leaking out and running down her cheeks. At last she sat up and reached for a tissue. After dabbing at her face and blowing her nose, she stood up and rebelted her bathrobe. Wallowing in grief wasn't going to get her anywhere. And it certainly wasn't her style. Even when she'd been in the depths of despair about her store, she hadn't been able to just sit around, feeling miserable.

It was still early and there was no chance of her finding oblivion in sleep for a long, long time, so after a stop in the bathroom to wash her face and rinse out her reddened eyes, she started down the hall to the kitchen. The shoe that she'd thrown at Jim was lying on the floor, its heel pointing upward as though in accusation. It would have served her right to stub her toe on it, she thought, reaching down to pick it up. After smoothing the leather with a thumb, she took the shoe back to the bedroom, then started for the kitchen again.

Terri had been going to fix herself a cup of tea. Instead, she experienced another pang of shock when she was greeted by the sight of two plates of uneaten cheesecake on the table. She'd forgotten all about them and had been so besotted earlier that she hadn't even noticed her green silk gown still lying in a sad little heap on the vinyl tile. Remembering with another knifelike twinge how Jim had ardently undressed her and then carried her into the bedroom, she picked up the crumpled garment and draped it over a kitchen chair. Then with a sigh she carried the plates of cheesecake to the sink with the other dirty dishes. Her stockroom might be a mess, but she'd never been the kind of person who could leave food drying on a plate. If she didn't get to the dishes now, they would just be worse in the morning. Mechanically she set to work.

A half hour later Terri set the last wineglass in the drainer and turned on the kettle. While the water boiled, she picked up the folder Jim had left. Her motives for doing so were not clear, even to herself. She supposed she was acting partly from remorse for the way she'd treated him and partly from a crazy desire to be closer to him by at least seeing what he'd been trying to tell her.

After bringing the papers and a cup of tea into the living room, she forced her eyes to focus, though they felt gritty, and began to study the material he'd prepared. It wasn't exactly escapist reading, and at first she had to work hard to concentrate. But at last she began to understand Jim's ideas. They were good—and tailored very specifically to her needs. Terri's remorse deepened. He must have spent hours putting this together. No wonder he'd been so excited about showing his work to her and so hurt when she'd brushed it aside. She'd convinced herself at the time that it was wholly inappropriate for him to shove business papers under her nose just after they'd made love. Now she realized that from his point of view it had been another kind of love offering.

Terri pressed her fingers against her forehead. It was throbbing so painfully that she got up to find some aspirin. Was there any way she could make amends for her callousness? she wondered as she uncapped the bottle and shook out two tablets.

After she'd washed them down with some water, she glanced at her watch. It was after eleven. Jim couldn't have been home for long, and she didn't imagine that he was going to be able to sleep any better than herself. She looked up his number in the phone book and then dialed with fingers that weren't quite steady. As she listened to the ringing on the other end of the line, she held her breath. But by the time she had counted to twelve, she knew that he either wasn't going to answer or for some reason hadn't gotten home yet. That realization set off a whole new train of worries. He'd been upset when he left her. Suppose he'd had an accident?

Terri jumped up and started to pace back and forth. The need to speak to Jim was suddenly overwhelming. But what should she do? He had to come home eventually, she told herself. What if she drove to his place and waited there? She opened the phone book again, searched once more for his listing and found his address. It was in a fashionable area of Alexandria—probably a town house, she surmised.

The decision made, she wrote down the address on a slip of paper and rushed back to her bedroom. There she got out a pair of jeans and a sweater. But she had barely stepped into her underwear when there was a loud knock at the door.

Terri frowned. It was almost midnight. Pulling on her robe once more, she started for the front door. She hadn't yet reached it when whoever was on the other side began to hammer loudly once again.

"Terri, I know you're in there, because your car's still in the parking lot."

The voice was Jim's, but the slurred delivery was one she'd never heard him use before. He sounded drunk.

She threw open the door just as the one across the hall opened. "Listen, buddy, don't you know it's after midnight?" her retired postal-worker neighbor growled. He was dressed in a bathrobe and slippers and had obviously been roused from his bed by all the noise. When he spotted Terri, he gave her a dirty look. "I'm going to—"

Terri didn't wait to hear the rest of the threat. Instead, she grabbed Jim by the arm and pulled him inside.

"Sorry 'bout that," he mumbled in an uneven voice when they were safely inside her apartment. "Hope you don't get thrown out on the street. Or maybe I do, because I don't think you should live here anymore." His cryptic words were accompanied by a wild laugh.

Terri gave him a sharp look. He swayed slightly on his feet, a lock of hair hung down over his forehead, and his bourbon-scented breath could have fueled a blowtorch. "You're drunk, aren't you?" she said.

"Yup," Jim agreed. "When I left, I didn't get any farther than Bernie's Tavern."

The place he'd mentioned was only two blocks from her apartment. She hoped he'd walked there and back.

"Needed to think things over," Jim muttered as he stumbled toward her couch and awkwardly sank down onto a cushion. "Wish I weren't having so much trouble talking. Something I have to say to you."

Terri stood over him with her hands on her hips. "And what is that?"

He gave her a bleary look, and she guessed he was having difficulty focusing. "That I love you too much to let your stupid pride mess things up for the two of us."

"My stupid pride?"

But apparently the speech had been all that Jim could manage. As Terri watched he slumped to one side and closed his eyes. Within moments he was snoring loudly.

"Oh, Jim, you can't just go to sleep on me like this," Terri murmured as she shook his shoulder. It was like trying to waken a dormant volcano. She wanted desperately to talk to him, but apparently that was hopeless. Sighing, she went to the linen closet for a blanket. After slipping off Jim's shoes, she propped a pillow under his head, covered him and stood looking down at his sleeping face. Then very gently she kissed his cheek and flipped off the light before making her way back down the hall to her room. As she settled herself in bed, she was sure she wouldn't be able to get to sleep. But when she closed her eyes, emotional exhaustion took over, and she slipped into oblivion.

* * *

Terri awoke the next morning to the aroma of freshly
brewed coffee. A moment later Jim appeared in the doorway with a tray. She opened her eyes wide. He'd apparently
been up for some time, because she could tell from the
droplets of water still in his hair that he'd showered. The
absence of the dark shadow that had roughened his jaw the
night before meant that he had also borrowed her razor.

"It's early and I hate to wake you, but we have to talk
before you go to your shop." As he walked toward her, the
expression on his face gave her no clue about what he intended to say, and her heart began to thump. Last night he'd
said he loved her. Had he meant it? And did he even remember that he'd said it?

After sitting down beside her, he laid the tray on the table next to the bed.

"Amaretto cheesecake for breakfast?" Terri commented
as she looked over at the two plates. There were also two
cups of the coffee she'd smelled.

"Why not? We didn't get around to it last night, and we
could both use something sweet."

Nodding, her eyes downcast, Terri picked up a fork and
cut herself a bite-size piece. Although she had no appetite,
she didn't want to refuse any more of Jim's offerings. He
watched carefully as she chewed and swallowed and then
took a sip of the hot coffee.

"Are you still mad at me?" he asked in a low voice.

"How could I be mad at a man who brings me cheesecake for breakfast?"

"Well, you might think he was crowding you."

Terri set down her cup and reached for his hand. "Oh,
Jim, I'm so sorry. You didn't deserve the way I treated you
last night."

His fingers curled around hers in a grip that was almost
painfully tight. "Even when I lashed out at you about that

loan?" He shook his head. "Terri, that was unforgivable
It's your right to get your financing wherever you want."

"What was unforgivable was my throwing that shoe a
you," she said in a small voice. "And even before I did that
I was using my brother's money as a weapon to lash out a
you. I think that after you left, I figured out why."

She was about to continue when he pressed gentle finger
against her lips.

"While we're both making confessions, there's some
thing I need to tell you. Maybe it will help you understan
where I've been coming from. I guess that after I stampe
out of here, I came to the conclusion that what happene
last night was my fault—and inevitable. Terri, from th
first, I didn't know how to act with you."

He cleared his throat. "I haven't told you much about m
marriage. But I suspect it has a lot to do with the way I'v
been treating you. Janet was a very dependent kind c
woman. She liked to be protected and have me make all th
big decisions, and that worked very well for the two of us
Even though I knew from the first that you were a very di
ferent kind of person, I just automatically fell back into ol
behavior patterns. I guess I loved you so much that
couldn't stand the thought of not riding in on a whit
charger and solving all your problems."

Terri felt tears spring to her eyes as she stared across th
bed at this man she loved so desperately. "A lot of wome
would kill to have a knight in shining armor like you com
along and solve their problems. My reaction was way out o
line, but I think I understand myself now. It was just that
was falling so deeply in love with you that it terrified me."

He stared at her. "Say that first part again, Terri. I wan
to make sure I heard you right."

She reached out and touched his cheek. "I love you, Jir
Holbrook, more than I thought I could love anyone."

"Terri, my God!" he cried, sweeping her into his arm
and crushing her against his chest. "You don't know wha
it does to me to hear you say that."

For a long time, they simply clung to each other. Then Terri tilted up her face so that she could look at him. "Being independent was so important to me that I couldn't function any other way. But then when I began to care about you so much that I knew I was never going to be really independent again, I was scared silly."

"It *is* scary to love someone," Jim agreed. "I've been self-sufficient for a long time, too. At first I wouldn't admit to myself that I couldn't live without you. But it was true from the first. It would kill me if I lost you now."

Terri shook her head. "Jim, you're never going to lose me."

"Is that a promise you're willing to make on a marriage contract?" Jim asked huskily.

Terri stared, struck dumb by his unexpected proposal.

"Before you answer that," Jim went on, "I want to make sure you know that I'm not asking you to give up anything that's important to you. I don't need a wife who stays home to cook and clean for me. I know being an independent businesswoman means a lot to you, and I wouldn't try to take that away."

"You're right. But it's never going to be more important to me than you are!" Terri cried as she threw her arms around his neck. "Oh, yes, Jim. I'll marry you. And that's the contract neither one of us will ever break."

His lips came down on hers, and she melted beneath him. Neither of them was able to think of anything but their newly acknowledged love and need for each other. And for the first time in three years, Terri didn't get around to opening her store until well past noon. But when she did, her face was wreathed in smiles.

* * * * *

Take 4 Silhouette Special Edition novels and a surprise gift
FREE

Then preview 6 brand-new books—delivered to your door as soon as they come off the presses! If you decide to keep them, you pay just $2.49 each*—a 9% saving off the retail price, *with no additional charges for postage and handling!*

Romance is alive, well and flourishing in the moving love stories of Silhouette Special Edition novels. They'll awaken your desires, enliven your senses and leave you tingling all over with excitement.

Start with 4 Silhouette Special Edition novels and a surprise gift absolutely FREE. They're yours to keep without obligation.   You can always return a shipment and cancel at any time.

Simply fill out and return the coupon today!

* Plus 69¢ postage and handling per shipment in Canada.

Silhouette Special Edition®

FOUR UNIQUE SERIES
FOR EVERY WOMAN YOU ARE...

Silhouette Romance

Love, at its most tender, provocative,
emotional...in stories that will make you laugh and
cry while bringing you the magic of falling in love.

6 titles per month

Silhouette Special Edition

Sophisticated, substantial and packed with
emotion, these powerful novels of life and love will
capture your imagination and steal your heart.

6 titles per month

Silhouette Desire

Open the door to romance and passion. Humorous,
emotional, compelling—yet always a believable
and sensuous story—Silhouette Desire never
fails to deliver on the promise of love.

6 titles per month

Silhouette Intimate Moments

Enter a world of excitement, of romance
heightened by suspense, adventure and the
passions every woman dreams of. Let us
sweep you away.

4 titles per month

 Silhouette Desire

COMING
NEXT MONTH

#403 FATE TAKES A HOLIDAY—Dixie Browning
Sophie Pennybaker won her all-too-attractive boss at a charity auction and was *forced* to go on a romantic vacation with him. It was fate . . . and the opportunity of a lifetime!

#404 GOLDEN PROMISE—Laurie Paige
When postperson Cynthia Robards literally came flying into Connor O'Shaugnessy's life, he wanted nothing to do with her. But she was determined to win him over and show him the golden promise of tomorrow.

#405 STAND BY ME—Nicole Monet
Beth Layton wanted to stand alone. But when an accident made her dependent on her handsome rescuer, she found two were stronger than one—and that compassion was only a step away from love.

#406 SHADOW WATCH—Sara Chance
Lacy Tipton and David Marsh pretended an affair to solve a crime—but when the case was wrapped up they both knew their feelings were more than a game.

#407 TROUBLED WATERS—Laura Taylor
Nick Andrews had jilted Kate Shaw at the altar. After eight long and lonely years, he knew he had to convince her that love could bridge their troubled waters.

#408 CHANGE OF HEART—Cathie Linz
After some hard lessons, Rebecca de Witt knew what she wanted in a man. Could Jake Fletcher—confirmed bachelor—convince her that he'd had a change of heart?

AVAILABLE NOW:

Silhouette Romance™
Legendary Lovers Trilogy

BY DEBBIE MACOMBER....

ONCE UPON A TIME, in a land not so far away, there lived a girl, Debbie Macomber, who grew up dreaming of castles, white knights and princes on fiery steeds. Her family was an ordinary one with a mother and father and one wicked brother, who sold copies of her diary to all the boys in her junior high class.

One day, when Debbie was only nineteen, a handsome electrician drove by in a shiny black convertible. Now Debbie knew a prince when she saw one, and before long they lived in a two-bedroom cottage surrounded by a white picket fence.

As often happens when a damsel fair meets her prince charming, children followed, and soon the two-bedroom cottage became a four-bedroom castle. The kingdom flourished and prospered, and between soccer games and car pools, ballet classes and clarinet lessons, Debbie thought about love and enchantment and the magic of romance.

One day Debbie said, "What this country needs is a good fairy tale." She remembered how well her diary had sold and she dreamed again of castles, white knights and princes on fiery steeds. And so the stories of Cinderella, Beauty and the Beast, and Snow White were reborn....

Look for Debbie Macomber's *Legendary Lovers* trilogy from Silhouette Romance: *Cindy and the Prince* (January, 1988); *Some Kind of Wonderful* (March, 1988); *Almost Paradise* (May, 1988). Don't miss them!